"I'm not involved with your son."

"Ben isn't happy," Mr. Haskell responded quietly.

Chloe's laugh was harsh. "You seem to think that Ben wants to see me, Mr. Haskell. He doesn't. He hates me. He hasn't forgiven me, and he told me he never will."

"That doesn't sound like indifference," Ben's father said. "It sounds like wounded pride."

She sighed. "What can I do? I can hardly chase after him when he walks away from me, can I?"

"Why not?"

Chloe stared at him, dumbfounded, and he smiled back at her, his eyes bright and mischievous.

"You aren't going to be as stubborn and unbending as my son," he said teasingly. "If you want him, go and get him."

If only things were that simple....

Books by Charlotte Lamb

A VIOLATION
SECRETS

HARLEQUIN PRESENTS

HARLEQUIN ROMANCE

These books may be available at your local bookseller.

Don't miss any of our special offers. Write to us at the following address for information on our newest releases.

Harlequin Reader Service
P.O. Box 52040, Phoenix, AZ   85072-2040
Canadian address: P.O. Box 2800, Postal Station A,
5170 Yonge St., Willowdale, Ont. M2N 6J3

CHARLOTTE LAMB

man hunt

Harlequin Books

TORONTO • NEW YORK • LONDON
AMSTERDAM • PARIS • SYDNEY • HAMBURG
STOCKHOLM • ATHENS • TOKYO • MILAN

Harlequin Presents first edition October 1985
ISBN 0-373-10827-3

Original hardcover edition published in 1985
by Mills & Boon Limited

Printed in U.S.A.

CHAPTER ONE

'I'VE changed my mind. I don't want to get married,' the bride said, cowering against her pillows.

Chloe put down the breakfast tray on the bedside table, her face calmly unsurprised. Jilly was given to springing moments of drama on her family; she was addicted to crisis, as her bridegroom must already have discovered.

'Okay, you can ring Tony and let him off the hook after you've eaten your breakfast.'

'Breakfast?' shrieked Jilly, fixing her aunt with an accusing eye, bright blue and humourless. 'It would make me sick. Take it away!'

'Your mother took a lot of trouble with it. Your last breakfast at home—she cried into the frying pan. The bacon is just how you like it, and it smells delicious.'

Jilly had inherited her emotional volatility from her mother; Dorry had always been given to mercurial swings of mood, the only predictable thing about either of them was that they would be quite unpredictable. Jilly had been on tenterhooks for months while she waited to get married; this last-minute panic was not surprising.

'Don't laugh at me!' Jilly muttered, sitting up as Chloe put the tray across her knees. 'I'm serious. What if I've made a mistake? What if it doesn't work out? I can't go through with it, I can't.'

'Don't you love Tony, after all?' Chloe enquired, suppressing her smile. Jilly's sense of humour had never extended to herself.

'I can't even remember what he looks like!' Jilly said, picking up her knife and fork in an absent-minded way. 'My mind's gone a blank.' As she bent her head her thick honey-blonde curls fell over her face. 'I've been awake all night, trying to remember what colour eyes he has,' she said with all the tragedy of Ophelia, then forked some bacon into her mouth. 'I've thought until my head aches,' she said as she swallowed it.

'Too much thinking can do that to you,' Chloe agreed, getting up. 'Watch breakfast TV for half an hour, that's always a useful way of doing absolutely no thinking at all. Drink your coffee while it's hot.' She switched on the TV set which was placed on a table facing the bed, and a voice began talking energetically, a second later followed by a face determined to be cheerful. Chloe moved to the door and Jilly said desperately: 'Don't go yet, don't leave me alone.'

'I can't stay long. You've no idea what the house is like down there, sheer bedlam. Your mother is running round in circles trying to work out what to do next; she's still in her nightie and dressing-gown and your father is refusing to put on that top hat, he says he looks an idiot in it.' Chloe came back to sit on the bed, though, her mind preoccupied with all the things she had to do before they left for the church. She was still in her own dressing-gown, an opulent blue Chinese housecoat, the colour of a kingfisher's wing, heavy satin, with a gold and green dragon curled around the jacket and tiny flowers sprinkled here and there. She had bought it in Hong Kong a year ago and only wore it on special occasions.

The television droned on and Jilly half-watched it, half ate. 'I wish there wasn't such a fuss,' she broke out as she put down her coffee cup a moment later. 'That's what I can't stand.'

'It will be over tomorrow.' Chloe was smiling and her niece gave her a fulminating glare, resenting her common sense.

'It will be too late by then! I keep trying to decide whether I really want to get married but I can't think straight especially with everyone rushing about and the house upside down. I didn't know getting married would be like this.'

Chloe ran a hand through her short, ruffled brown hair; suppressing a sigh. 'You seemed sure enough a week ago.' She was understating the case; Jilly had been wildly insistent on marrying Tony for the past three months, ever since she announced her engagement and wouldn't budge in spite of the protests of her anxious parents. Chloe hadn't said much, just listened, finding the spectacle of her niece's latest drama as amusing as she had found most of the scenes which had gone before it. Jilly was a source of constant amusement to her, the nineteen years of her life had been crowded with incident. She was a girl to whom things happened, and if they didn't Jilly compensated for that, too; one thing she hated was a quiet life, she somehow managed to *make* things happen, if there was a lull in the ceaseless storm which had surrounded her since she was born.

'I can't remember how I felt a week ago,' Jilly wailed, pushing away the tray.

Chloe picked it up before it fell on to the carpet, spilling coffee and marmalade all over the soft white carpet. Jilly had a pretty bedroom, her parents were well-off and had given her everything she could want, and maybe that was what was wrong with her. She was a spoilt only child of doting parents and in no way ready for the reality of married life. Tony wasn't rich, although he might be one day. He had a good job and a pleasantly furnished flat in which they would live, but he wasn't going to be able to give Jilly the sort of background she was accustomed to.

'Well, you'd better make up your mind pretty fast. There are only two hours before the car arrives,' Chloe said, moving to the door.

'Two hours!'

'Just time to have your bath and get dressed,' Chloe added, her hazel eyes teasing.

'I can't go through with it!' Jilly began drumming her heels in her bed in exactly the way she had always drummed them when her mother tried to make her go to school. She hadn't changed much since then, thought Chloe.

'Your mother will be up soon to help you get into your wedding dress.' Chloe ignored her, opening the door, the tray balanced on her slim hip. Under the satin dressing gown her body was gracefully supple; she was a tall woman with high breasts and long legs, a sensual way of moving which compensated for her cool, unexciting face. Her nature was expressed in her features, her humour in the glint of her hazel eyes, her down to earth common sense in the firm line of her mouth and the strong-minded curve of her chin.

'You're going to be a ravishing bride,' she coaxed but stopped as Jilly gave a sharp gasp. 'What's wrong now?' she asked, looking back with resignation.

Jilly pointed a finger at the television, threw her aunt a distinctly anxious look, then snatched her hand down and clutched at the bedclothes.

'What is it?' Chloe asked, taking a few steps backward so that she could see the television. She hadn't been listening to the relentless chatter; it had merely been living wallpaper which she had hoped might soothe Jilly back into a cheerful state of mind.

'Nothing,' Jilly said in a strained voice, but from her expression doom had just come upon her. Chloe stared at the screen and saw a shot of Venice—a pale pink palazzo, a glittering stretch of blue canal, a black gondola skimming out of view. She couldn't see anything there to make Jilly look stricken.

'Switch if off!' Jilly said urgently.

Puzzled, Chloe walked towards the screen. Venice vanished, and back in the studio the anchor man began talking again. 'This morning we have the managing director of the Luxor

Hotels Chain in the studio to talk about this new venture. Mr Ben Haskell is . . .' Chloe almost dropped the tray, everything on it rattled as she clutched at it, stumbling, her skin suddenly pale.

A face had filled the screen; strong features, with heavy lids half-veiling cool eyes which seemed to stare straight at her and through her, a long arrogant nose and a firmly controlled mouth. She didn't wait to hear his voice, she shot a hand out to flick the switch and the face disappeared slowly until all that was left was a white dot on the grey glass.

'I think I'll have my bath now,' Jilly said unsteadily, clambering out of bed; and vanished before her aunt could get a good look at her face.

'Oh, hell!' Chloe said aloud, with ferocity, feeling like hurling the tray at the television. Why did *he* have to be on television that morning of all mornings? No wonder Jilly had looked as if she'd gone into acute shock! Chloe felt her own ears buzzing with hypertension, she swallowed and followed her niece out of the room.

At the bottom of the stairs she met her sister who gave her a distracted stare as though not sure who she was; Dorry was in a state of total disorientation.

'Jilly's in the bathroom. Shouldn't you be getting ready? It's gone nine.'

'I know that!' Dorry sounded as if she was on the point of screaming. 'Clive's been driving me crazy. He says he'll carry that damned hat but he won't be seen wearing it. You talk to him, Chloe, he listens to you—and try to stop Mother from bullying the bridesmaids, one of them is nearly in tears, Mother made her do her hair again because she said it didn't look right with the dresses.' Dorry ran a hand over her carefully coiffeured hair. She should have had a large family, she was a motherly creature, full fleshed and rounded, warm and ripely coloured with thick fair hair in loose waves and eyes exactly like her daughter's, their blue inclined to over brightness and too often filling with tears. 'Will you ring the caterers and check that . . .'

'Yes, I'll do that now.'

'And you'd better make sure the bridal cars are going to be here on time. Clive ought to do that but he has gone off to sulk in the garden. If you see him in the greenhouse stop him getting himself dirty before we have to leave. He'll be digging in that morning suit if we don't watch him.' Dorry was trying to think of too many things at once and envisaging the worst, her eyes distracted. 'And could you check that the flowers have been delivered? The carnations for button-holes should be here by ten.'

'Okay. Go and have your bath, there's Jilly coming out of the bathroom now. Get in while you can.'

Dorry nodded then ran an eye over Chloe, frowning. 'You aren't dressed yet!'

'I will be, don't worry about it. Do you want me to help Jilly or . . .'

'No,' Dorry said at once. 'I'll do that.' She had never been able to have another child after Jilly was born, something had gone wrong and she had been warned never to have any more babies. She had poured all her considerable maternal passion into her one child. That was why Jilly had been so spoiled.

Chloe went into the kitchen and deposited the tray. Her mother wandered in from the room where the bridesmaids were gathered, their excited voices filling the downstairs of the house. Jilly had wanted three of her best friends; she had around a dozen 'best friends'. She had been the most popular girl in her school, people instinctively liked her, her flare for drama spilled over everyone else around her and made life more interesting, and she had qualities which went beyond that. She was generous, lively, affectionate and loving, she flung herself into whatever she did with more verve than most people ever have. She attracted people like a candle flame attracts moths.

'Where is Dorry?' asked Hetty Tyrrell, sitting down. She had reached the stage in life where she sat down every time she saw a chair; she always got up again a moment later and got busy doing whatever came to hand but the energy which in Jilly burned so high had become in her grandmother a carefully nursed flame.

'Getting dressed. Do you feel like some coffee, Mother? I'm just going to make myself some.' Chloe spooned instant coffee granules into two cups while the kettle boiled, then picked up the phone and dialled the florist's number. Her mother got up and made a little foray into the garden to quarrel with Clive.

'You'll get mud all over your trousers, come

back indoors and don't be so silly!' she yelled as she came back into the kitchen, slamming the door. 'He really is a maddening man, I don't know why Dorry married him.'

Chloe smiled absently as she rang the caterers and made sure that the food would be delivered on schedule.

Hetty sat down with a tired sigh. 'I shall be very glad when today is over. Such a fuss. Anyone would think nobody had ever got married before. Dorry couldn't organise a dolls' tea party.' She was up again before she had finished talking. 'That kettle's boiling. I'll make the coffee.'

'No, I will,' Chloe said, replacing the phone and whirling. 'Sit down, Mother.'

Reluctantly, her mother sat. She was shorter than either of her daughters, her once fair hair a fine silvery shade now, her face still smooth but her neck lined and wrinkled above the chic powder blue dress she was wearing. She was very thin and upright, still stylish and eye-catching for all her sixty-seven years, and she had several admirers in tow, although she seemed reluctant to get married again. She had been a widow for ten years, it had, perhaps, become a habit to her; at the moment she had both freedom and choice of male escorts on social occasions. The real passion of her life was bridge, which she played several times a week with unhidden ferocity and concentration, and she picked her bridge partners with as much care as if she meant to marry one of them.

Chloe took the coffee over to her and Hetty got out her powder compact to look at herself wryly. 'Blue's such a cold colour, maybe I should have worn pink. How I hate my neck—it looks like an elephant's trunk! When I've drunk this coffee I'll go up and see Jilly in her lovely dress. If I'm going to cry I'd rather do it in private! Then I can wash my face and do my make-up again before I'm seen in public.' She snapped the compact shut and slid it into her bag, picking up her coffee cup. 'This should be your wedding day, not Jilly's,' she said ruthlessly, ignoring her daughter's wry grimace. 'Twenty-five! You're leaving it too late, Chloe. A career is all very fine, but don't you want to have babies?'

'I think I'll take my coffee upstairs,' Chloe said, making for the door. She had heard that particular lecture too many times, she knew it by heart.

'You can go on singing after you're married,' her mother shrieked after her with the indifference to pitch of the half-deaf who refuse to admit that they are hard of hearing. 'They ruin your skin, you know.'

Chloe halted, bemused by that, and in spite of herself dying to know what her mother meant by it. 'What ruins your skin? Babies? Or singing?' she enquired with fond amusement.

'Night-clubs,' her mother said in a voice which could shatter glass at fifty paces. Chloe laughed and fled before Hetty said any more.

Her family had never approved of her career; they were suspicious about the sort of people she probably met, and worried about a life-style so far from their own. They were not night birds; they went to bed early and got up at unearthly hours while Chloe was still fast asleep. A night-club, to them, was a place other people went to—the sort of people they did not want to meet. Chloe had explained until she was blue in the face that she did a perfectly respectable job and worked very hard at it. They would never believe her, they preferred their own garish picture of night-club life. They hated her music, too. Jazz was a discordant jangle to them, but then they were not very musical. Hetty had a weak spot for lush, romantic music with a million strings and a saccherine-drowned tune. Dorry was simply tone deaf; she didn't hear music at all and to hear her humming was to suffer if you had any sense of pitch at all.

It had not been easy to persuade Dorry to let Gil come to the wedding reception. 'A night-club pianist?' Dorry had repeated in round-eyed dismay. 'What would Tony's parents think?'

'Don't be absurd, Dorry, nobody will faint when they see Gil. He doesn't smoke hash or wear spangled suits,' Chloe had said, but she had made a mistake in being so explicit, she had put Dorry's vague worries into words which her sister gabbled back at her.

'Hash? Spangled suits? Oh, Chloe, that's what I mean—Tony's family will get such a bad impression of us all. They haven't met you yet, I don't want them to get the idea that . . .'

'That what?' demanded Chloe, fixing her with

a deadly eye, and Dorry backed down after a moment because she had enough worries over the wedding arrangements, she didn't want to have a stand-up fight with her sister, too.

'Oh, well,' she said after a pause for thought, 'We might as well have a look at him, I suppose—at least we'll know the worst.' Then she had added: 'I hope he's nothing like the last man you brought here!' and Chloe's face had stiffened and turned pale.

Dorry had seen her expression and hurriedly dropped the hot coal she had incautiously picked up. She had learnt long ago that the fifteen years between herself and her sister did not give her *carte blanche* to say exactly what she liked. Dorry had always had a tendency to say the first thing that came into her head, blurting out what others would more wisely have left unsaid, and even as a little girl Chloe had had a way of looking at her that made Dorry nervous. Perhaps because she was the youngest in a spaced-out family, Chloe had learnt to defend herself and her little patch of personal territory at an early age.

'What's the Gil short for?' Dorry had asked, to cover her tracks, and Chloe had looked blank.

'I've no idea, it hadn't occurred to me. I must ask him.'

It was seeing Dorry whirling around the crowded hotel ballroom in which the reception was being held that later reminded Chloe of their conversation. She looked up at Gil's amused face as he nibbled a sausage on a stick.

'What's Gil short for?' she asked him and he made a distasteful face.

'Don't ask!'

'I just did. Let me guess—Gilbert?'

'I wish it was.' He looked around the room. 'Your family is terrifying—everyone I meet seems to be related to you. The groom and his family look pretty harassed. They're definitely in the minority here, aren't they?'

Chloe laughed, glancing around, too, and recognising most of the faces. 'Tony is certainly taking on something,' she agreed.

'His bride is a knock-out,' Gil said, staring at Jilly in her traditional white silk and lace gown, the veil thrown back over her blonde curls and her small face flushed with excitement and triumph. 'A knock-out,' repeated Gil.

Chloe recognised his expression; men had always stared at Jilly with that sort of interest. Her parents hadn't needed to spoil he; life was going to do that anyway. Jilly had been a knock-out even in her school uniform she had managed to make the blue gymslip and white ankle socks look like some sexy outfit meant to turn men on—and it had certainly done that. Chloe's frown carved deep lines in her normally smooth forehead as she watched her niece dancing with her new husband, laughing up at him with those instinctively provocative blue eyes.

'Hey! Why the scowl?' Gil's voice broke into her thoughts and she looked round blankly at him.

'Sorry, I was miles away. What did you say?'

'Let's dance,' Gil said, putting down his glass. He was a head taller than Chloe and settled his cheek against her hair as they began to dance, his arm loosely holding her waist. 'Are they going to ask you to sing?' he murmured. 'Am I here to play for my supper?'

'Our sort of music wouldn't fit,' Chloe smiled. She watched the young band playing at the far end of the room. 'They aren't at all bad,' she thought aloud and Gil shot a look in their direction, shrugging his thin shoulders.

'If you like this sort of stuff,' he accepted with faint disdain. Gil was a man with a one-track mind, he was intensely involved with his own style of playing and one of the best jazz pianists in London. When he wasn't seated at his piano his personality was vague and absent-minded, even his hair was pale above his unmemorable face. When you weren't with him you couldn't quite remember what he looked like. Gil only came to life when he played. Then his eyes burnt with feeling, diamond bright, his body flowed with his music and people watched him excitedly, but once he took his fingers from the keys he slackened into sleepy insignificance again.

'Weddings depress me,' he said into her hair.

'Did you cry in church?' Chloe teased and he grinned down at her.

'No, but I felt like it. Half the women seemed to be using hankies. I was relieved you didn't cry, you're not the crying type, are you?' His eyes were faintly curious; although they worked together frequently their relationship never developed past a warm friendship. Gil didn't have any energy left over from his music and Chloe wasn't attracted to him sexually.

'No,' Chloe agreed. She found it hard to cry, she would rather laugh even when she was badly hurt. She hated to show her feelings, the deeper something went the more she tried to hide her reactions.

'You're an odd creature,' Gil said drily.

'Aren't we all?' she shrugged, watching her sister dancing with poor Clive in his morning suit and hangdog expression. He had hated being forced into that gear, he was a man who liked a quiet life. What on earth had made him marry Dorry whose life had never been quiet? The lure of the opposite? His marriage couldn't have been dull, anyway, living with Dorry was a constant see-saw between one emotion and another.

Chloe's gaze moved on to where Jilly and Tony were dancing. How lovely Jilly looked and how predictable that she had picked a young man with something very like her father's steady, stable temperament. Obviously the combination worked. One thing was certain—Tony was crazy about his new wife, he couldn't take his eyes off her upturned, smiling face and Jilly looked glowing, radiant.

'Why the sigh?' Gil asked and Chloe forced a smile.

'Envy, maybe. Jilly is walking on the ceiling, isn't she?' Her mind went back to that morning; Jilly's irrational fears about getting married, the incredible coincidence of seeing Ben Haskell on breakfast TV. She half closed her eyes, angry with herself for still caring. Damn him. She refused to think about him, it infuriated her when her emotions wouldn't stay under control.

She hadn't cried when she heard the wedding music pealing and saw her niece floating down the aisle with the veil over her face and her hand clasped tightly in her father's, but a hard lump had come up in Chloe's throat and she had had to look down for a second. She had heard Dorry sniffing and their mother blowing her nose; emotion briefly filled the church as men cleared their throats and the organ clamoured in triumph.

'Barbaric ceremonies,' Gil said and Chloe laughed.

'Weddings? Positively primitive. The tribe gathers and the ritual can't be altered or everyone gets very superstitious and predicts bad luck. We aren't so very far from the Dark Ages, are we?'

'As the crow flies,' Gil nodded solemnly and they both chuckled, then in a flurry of white lace and swishing skirts Jilly was there, hugging her aunt and whispering.

'Come and help me change into my going-away outfit!'

Chloe was surprised. 'What about your mother?' she asked. Dorry would be hurt, didn't her niece realise that? This was Dorry's hour; she had put weeks of hard work into her daughter's wedding day, Jilly couldn't ask someone else to help her get changed.

'I want to talk to you,' Jilly said with an

urgency that puzzled. She threw Gil a charming, indifferent smile. 'Hi, nice to see you, I hope you're having a good time?' Gil wasn't her type, though, he was far too quiet, and his wry smile acknowledged that.

'Be happy,' he said casually but Chloe saw his eyes and was touched by their gentle warmth. Gil was a nice man.

'Thanks,' Jilly said equally, handing him another dazzling smile, then put her arm around her aunt. 'Come *on*, Chloe! I haven't got much time and there's something I have to say to you.'

Two rooms had been reserved on the first floor of the hotel so that bride and groom could change before driving off to catch their plane to Barbados. Chloe watched Jilly take off her veil and throw it on to the bed. Unzipping the white dress, Chloe helped her niece step out of it.

'Isn't it fabulous?' Jilly asked, watching Chloe hang it up. 'I'm going to have it altered into an evening dress; a lower neckline and no sleeves and it will be perfect.' Standing in front of the dressing-table mirror in her long white silk slip Jilly ran a hand over her hair, her eyes on her aunt. 'Chloe . . .'

'Yes?' Chloe was carefully folding the veil between tissue paper and placing it into the empty suitcase which Dorry would collect later.

'I'm so happy,' Jilly said abruptly, her arms lifted in an excited gesture. 'Really, it was crazy the way I felt this morning—I love Tony and everything is going to be wonderful. I just had butterflies this morning, I didn't mean any of it.'

'I realised that,' Chloe said with loving amusement, turning to smile at her. 'Is that all you wanted to say, for heaven's sake?'

Jilly turned away, very flushed, and began pulling her slip off. Chloe moved to help, taking it away to put into the suitcase on top of the veil. Jilly hovered, watching, looking incredibly young in her brief panties and bra.

'I've got to tell you,' she burst out. 'This morning when I saw him on television I . . .'

'Forget him,' Chloe said harshly. 'Don't let him spoil your wedding day, he isn't worth it.' She had turned pale again and her hands trembled as she packed the slip deftly, her back to her niece.

'You don't understand!'

'I do, Jilly. I wish I hadn't turned on that damned set, it upset you.'

'It reminded me, that's all,' Jilly said and Chloe turned to look at her with compunction. She was so young, for all her sophisticated chatter; she had no control over her vacillating emotions, her moods fluctuated like the tide pulled by the inconstant moon. Did she really think she was ready for marriage? Chloe felt a stab of anxiety for her.

'I'm sorry if it spoiled your day, Jilly. You'd forgotten all about him. I could kick myself for having switched on that set.'

'I hadn't forgotten,' Jilly denied in a quick gabble, very flushed. 'It's been at the back of my mind all the time. I've tried to tell you, Chloe, but I'm such a coward, I couldn't get the words out.'

Chloe stared at her, thinking hard. 'Are you feeling guilty, Jilly?' she guessed gently. That didn't surprise her, she could easily work out why. No doubt Jilly had flirted with him, used those provocative blue eyes on him with a woman's instincts driving her sixteen-year-old body, and perhaps in a court of law a judge might see Jilly's tantalising manner as some excuse for what happened later, but Chloe angrily rejected that idea. Jilly had been a child, playing an adult game without fully realising what she was doing. Chloe could forgive her. She couldn't forgive the man who had taken advantage of Jilly's immaturity.

'Yes,' Jilly said with a long sigh of relief. 'Terribly. I didn't mean to hurt you, Chloe, I felt dreadful when all the fuss started and I saw what I'd done to you.'

'Forget it,' Chloe said quickly, frowning. She had tried so hard to hide the damage done to her, she winced at the thought of Jilly's understanding. 'It was three years ago, it doesn't matter any more, you ought to put it behind you, forget it ever happened. Come on, we have to get you dressed. You don't want to keep Tony waiting, do you?'

'Don't talk to me as if I was a child!' Jilly burst out, trembling, and facing her aunt with her hands clenched at her sides. 'I can't go away with Tony without getting it straight with you, I hate myself.'

Chloe was taken aback by her niece's vehemence. She froze, the chic little coral pink suit

which Jilly would wear to go on honeymoon held
out to her. A spark of intuition leapt between
them and Chloe slowly backed and sat down on
the bed.

'I didn't know what to do, you see,' Jilly
muttered, looking like someone facing a firing
squad. 'It never entered my head that Cherry
would tell anyone, it was a secret and we never
told on each other. That summer holidays Cherry
had a boyfriend who had a motorbike, she was
always going off with him, riding pillion, and I
suppose I was jealous. I didn't have a boyfriend
and I felt out of it.'

She looked almost exactly as she had three
years ago, a slender girl with small, high breasts
and a tiny waist, her blonde hair surrounding a
pretty, rather self-willed face. Chloe was listening
with an intensity that made her head ache. She
hardly breathed.

'I guess I wanted to knock the grin off Cherry's
face,' Jilly kept her chin up and her eyes fixed on
her aunt, pleading in them. 'She was so pleased
with herself for getting one up on me.' She took a
long breath. 'So . . . so I told her that Ben had
made love to me. He was so dishy, Cherry and I
had got a bit of a crush on him, I knew it would
make her jealous, and it did. She wouldn't believe
me at first, so I had to make up all sorts of details
to sound convincing and then she did believe me,
and she was as mad as I'd wanted her to be, but I
hadn't dreamt that she'd go and tell her mother
or that Mrs Hunt would rush off and ring my
Mum to warn her what was going on. Honestly,

Chloe, I didn't mean to start that sort of row, but when it blew up I was so scared I had to go on lying. Mum got Cherry there, I couldn't back down in front of Cherry, she'd have laughed at me. I'd never have lived it down.'

'Are you telling me it was all lies?' Chloe's voice was hoarse with shock.

'Yes.' Jilly had backed away, as if afraid Chloe was going to hit her.

'Ben didn't make a pass at you?' Chloe's head was spinning dizzily as she took in everything it meant—she couldn't believe it. Jilly had lied? It hadn't occurred to her—then or now—that Jilly could have invented the whole story.

Jilly shook her head, her eyes fixed on Chloe's white face. 'I'm sorry, I didn't mean to cause so much trouble. Once I'd started lying I didn't seem able to stop. I kept hoping it would all blow over, but everyone got so upset about it. Honestly, it hadn't dawned on me how complicated things could get until it was too late.'

'Too late?' Chloe repeated in a shaking voice. 'My God, what do you mean, too late? You accused Ben of making a pass at you. You called him a liar when he denied it. Your father nearly called the police—and now you say it was too late to tell the truth?'

'I didn't mean it to happen,' Jilly pleaded. 'If everyone hadn't got so worked up I might have come clean, but can't you see—I didn't dare? Mum was crying, Dad was shouting, you were looking as if the sky had just fallen in—I couldn't admit I'd made it all up.'

Chloe sat down suddenly. 'Ben said you were lying. He said it was pure imagination.' She closed her eyes, remembering his taut, darkly flushed face; the searing rage in his blue eyes. She had looked at him with contempt and Ben had stared back at her as if he had never seen her before. All the colour had slowly drained out of his face at that moment, and his mouth had stiffened into a hard, bitter line. 'I didn't believe him,' she whispered. She shivered, so cold her skin had goose pimples. Her jaws were aching, she felt her teeth grinding together and the jar of the movement made her head throb.

She opened her eyes to look at Jilly and the girl flinched as if Chloe had hit her. 'Don't look at me like that! I'm so sorry, Chloe, I wish it hadn't happened. I saw your face this morning, when he was on the television—and I felt sick. I knew I had to tell you the truth. I've often tried to get up the nerve to tell you, but it never seemed the right time.'

Chloe stood up stiffly. She didn't feel she really knew her niece at all. Jilly had tears in her eyes now, but she had cried three years ago, her trembling fingers over her face. None of them had really doubted Jilly's word; Ben's denials had merely made them angrier. Jilly didn't tell lies, they had told Ben icily, she wasn't the type. Jilly was their golden girl— frank, open, spilling with excitement. She wasn't secretive or mean—why on earth should she invent such a story? She hadn't even told her parents in the beginning, she had confided in a friend, she had been so shocked and anxious. It hadn't occurred to them that Jilly's love of drama might make her invent the incident to impress Cherry—and it was true that Jilly did not lie as a general rule, she merely embroidered and exaggerated. The very fact that she hadn't done so over Ben had made it all the more impossible for them to doubt her. Jilly had played it down, been hesitant—and they had been utterly convinced by that.

Ben had given them a cool, dry stare before he left. Chloe had deciphered that look as insolent mockery and burned with anger.

'I'd watch her if I were you,' he had said, shrugging as though admitting everything. 'She's going to give you a lot of trouble.'

That had been adding insult to injury, they had taken him to mean something very different to what Chloe now saw he had meant. His eyes had been blue ice as he gave Chloe a final glance. Clive had followed him to the door, issuing threats should he ever show his face again.

'Don't worry, you won't see me again,' Ben had said tersely.

The front door had slammed, Clive had come back, making a gesture oddly like someone washing his hands. 'That's the end of that,' he had said and put his arms around his daughter. 'My poor baby,' he had said and Jilly had clung to him, crying.

She was crying now. 'Say you forgive me, Chloe—I had to come clean or my whole marriage would seem like a lie.' She lifted her head, her face smeared with tears, her mouth trembling. 'You understand, don't you, Chloe?'

Chloe stared at her blankly.

'Chloe? Say something.' Jilly's voice quavered, she took a step nearer.

'Understand? No, Jilly, I don't understand,' Chloe said slowly. 'But right now you have to get dressed. Tony will be waiting. You'd better wash your face and make yourself look normal, although God knows what that means where you're concerned.' She stopped as Jilly gave a stifled sob. 'I'll send your mother up,' she said in a dry voice and walked out of the room on unsteady legs. She felt oddly sea-sick, like someone who has been on a boat for a long time and can't orientate herself on dry land. Her knees trembled, she lurched and caught at the banister.

Dorry was coming up the stairs. 'Isn't she ready yet?'

'You'd better go and talk to her,' Chloe managed in a drained voice.

Her sister did a double-take. 'What's wrong?' Her voice rose sharply. 'Is something wrong with Jilly?' Without waiting for an answer she rushed past Chloe towards the room she had just left, and Chloe slowly went on down stairs, wondering if Jilly would tell her mother what she had just told *her*.

The noise of the reception reached her like a hurricane as she got to the lobby. She couldn't face them all, particularly her mother. Hetty would read her face; Chloe knew that her mother had a talent for noticing precisely what one did not want her to see. She walked out of the hotel, shivering in the fresh spring wind. She had no coat, her pink dress was far too thin.

How could Jilly have done it? The way Cherry told the story, they had all been given the impression that Ben had practically raped Jilly and when they carefully tried to find out exactly what Ben had done Jilly had covered her face and cried, and they had all been desperately sorry for her. Poor Jilly, they had thought, horrified by what they imagined, and they had looked at Ben with angry contempt. They had believed him guilty before he opened his mouth. Ben had been the outsider—and the Tyrrells had always been a united family. They had closed ranks against him.

How must he have felt? He had looked searchingly at Chloe and she had stared back with a contempt she didn't try to hide and a pain she refused to let him see. Her emotions had been in a tangle—sexual jealousy had been mixed with her other reactions. Jilly had been so pretty, even at sixteen; her blue eyes so innocently inviting, her mouth with an unmistakably sensual curve. Of course, at the time, Chloe wouldn't admit even to herself that she was jealous, such an idea would have been too humiliating, but she had known that Jilly had a sexual attraction she didn't have. Jilly was teasing and provocative where Chloe was cool and faintly withdrawn on the surface. Jilly might have been half a child—but she had also been half a woman.

Chloe's feelings had been charged with far more than the sheet outrage that the rest of the family had felt.

She stood by her car, not even sure how she had got there. She didn't think about Gil, or her puzzled family. She couldn't remember walking across the car park, she didn't know what she meant to do. She was in shock. Her fingers shook as she searched her bag for her car keys. She unlocked the car and got into it, still shivering. She was so cold, she leaned over and got an old suede car coat from the back seat where she had flung it the day before. It was too shabby to wear except when she was walking in the forest or working on the car. Huddled in it, she felt slightly warmer. She started the engine and almost took the wing off the car parked in front, she had to swerve to avoid it, her tyres screeching on the car-park gravel.

She drove away, her brows creased in pain. Jilly's confession had come out of the blue, what would it do to the rest of the family? No doubt they'd find excuses for Jilly but Chloe didn't feel she could forgive her. Jilly had been prepared to blacken a man's character, destroy Chloe's happiness, distress her parents—and all for what? So that she shouldn't lose face with a school-friend!

Chloe felt sick the more she thought about it. Realising that you had been deceived about someone made you feel as though the ground had been cut from under your feet. Chloe felt afraid. She had blithely imagined that she knew her niece inside out and she had been so wrong; it undermined your faith in yourself to realise something like that. Jilly had dropped a bombshell—and the fall-out had only just begun.

She halted at some traffic lights, her eyes absently fixed on them. The red became a glowing amber, then green, and she drove on without having any real idea where she was going.

She hadn't seen Ben since, except that morning on the television. Whenever she thought about him she had felt a painful bitterness, he had hurt her more than she would ever have admitted to anyone. She slowed, frowning. But he hadn't, of course—Ben had been innocent, it had been Jilly who was lying. She still hadn't realised all the implications of what she had heard. She had to start seeing Ben differently again. Three years ago Jilly had shown her a side of Ben she had not expected—and today she had reversed that image and Chloe had to unpeel three years of bitter lesion and see Ben the way she had before Jilly sprang her first surprise. Although what did it matter? Ben had been out of her life for three years, she would never see him again, and if she ever did he probably wouldn't care to speak to her. His eyes had been so angry the last time they looked at her, and it was too late now to apologise, or explain, or tell him she knew he had told the truth.

Her brows jerked together and her hands tightened on the wheel—too late? The phrase had a bitterly familiar ring; wasn't that what Jilly had kept saying? Chloe had angrily rejected the words when Jilly said them, but now she was using them herself and weren't they just as much of an excuse now? She had taken her niece's side against Ben, she shared Jilly's guilt. Wasn't that how Ben would see it? He had been angrier with her than with Jilly. He had had a right to expect Chloe to listen to *him*, not her niece, to believe him and be on his side. But she hadn't. She had been deeply in love with Ben—yet she had immediately swallowed Jilly's story almost as though she had been expecting it—and in a sense she had been expecting it.

The way she had felt about Ben had been too deep, there had been fear mixed with her love. She had anticipated losing him because it had all seemed too good to be true. She hadn't known him very long anyway. He had come into a night-club where she was singing and sat with half a dozen people at a table close to the stage. Chloe had noticed him immediately, how could she miss a man who looked like Ben? He had watched her as though he knew her, the blue smoke of a cigar curling round his head. Chloe had felt weak at the knees each time she met the lazy intimacy of his eyes, and she hadn't really been too surprised to find him in the club again the following night. That time he had been alone and he had sent her a note asking her to have supper with him when she had finished her act. Chloe had been in love almost before they actually met; she had fallen in love with an immediacy that terrified her, especially when she managed to think clearly and realised how little she knew about this stranger who seemed so familiar.

Dragging herself out of her memories she looked around her blindly and was suddenly aware of where she was—she had driven without an idea of where she was going, her body on automatic pilot. Now with a shock of disbelief she saw that she had unerringly found her way to the Mayfair street where Ben lived. A car behind her hooted impatiently as she stared up at his house, her car stationary, and Chloe hurriedly edged her way into a parking space right opposite the white façade she remembered so well.

She sat with her hands on the wheel, staring at it, her stomach lurching. Had she known where she was going? At one level of her mind she had told herself she was just driving blindly, but she had been lying to herself. Ever since it dawned on her that Jilly had lied she had been possessed with a desperate need to see Ben again, explain, apologise.

Would he care? Three years is a long time, she thought; anything could have happened in Ben's life since I last saw him. He could be married. Her fingertips became moist with perspiration at that idea. She couldn't bear to think about that. He could have moved, she thought, instead, he might have forgotten her. He might not want to see her again even when she had explained— could she blame him if he walked away, shrugging his indifference?

Her heart was beating so hard she felt giddy. She wanted to see him again—the very thought of it was making her weak and her reactions frightened her, had always frightened her, she couldn't bear the piercing love she felt for Ben. Chloe had always believed that she would love quietly, calmly—she was too down to earth to be happy with extreme emotion. Loving Ben had been like driving a powerful car you can't control—a car whose brakes don't work. Chloe had felt she was facing disaster, she had fallen irretrievably in love with a stranger and because she did not know Ben well enough to be sure of anything about him, she hadn't been sure whether or not he could have done what Jilly had accused him of doing.

She sat for minutes on end, her eyes fixed on the house, trying to make up her mind what to do. She was about to drive off in despair when the front door opened.

CHAPTER TWO

Two men came into view on the stone steps, one of them was a bowed old man in an astrakhan-collared coat, his thin silvery hair blowing slightly in the wind—the other was Ben, and it was at him that Chloe stared, so intent on him that she was scarcely aware of herself or concerned in case he noticed her. He had changed in so many small ways; his dark hair was styled differently; he wore it shorter than he had, his face was thinner; the angles at cheek and jaw sharper and more forbidding, the upward slant of his brows a sardonic line above those vivid blue eyes. Ben had always been a strong man, now that strength had hardened into force. Every line in his face and body spoke of an implacable determination.

Chloe frowned, sinking lower in her seat. She didn't want him to see her. If she had met this man, looking the way he did, would she have looked twice at him? The man she remembered had had warmth and humour; he hadn't emanated power the way Ben visibly did now.

She shot another look towards the two men as they slowly came down the steps. A gleaming silver limousine was drawn up at the kerb outside the house. A chauffeur in a dark green uniform slid out of it, sprang to open the passenger door

and stood holding it, his face attentive. The old
man was talking vigorously to Ben who listened,
his head bent towards him, nodding whenever
the other paused to draw breath. Chloe had never
met any of Ben's family, but she had seen
photographs of them. Ben's home was liberally
scattered with silver-framed photographs. She
felt sure she had seen the old man's face before.
Or was it a family resemblance she recognised?
Wasn't this Ben's father? He was much shorter,
but then his narrow shoulders were stooped and
his white head sunk forward. His body seemed
frail in the heavy overcoat. Chloe got the
impression that Ben's hand continually hovered
close to the old man's elbow, as though ready to
catch him if he stumbled yet not wishing to be
obvious about it. If there was pride in Ben's face,
that was echoed in the older man whose lined,
austere features were fiercely proud, he was
silently rejecting any help from Ben, holding
himself carefully as he grasped the top of the car,
leaning on it and turning to go on talking.

Ben's head lifted, he glanced casually around
while he listened. One hand raked back a
windblown swathe of black hair, then his gaze
briefly touched Chloe's car, moving on without
pause before he did a double-take, his eyes
swiftly moving back to her. Chloe looked away,
her cheeks burning. She was so flustered she put
out a trembling hand and switched on the
ignition, hardly conscious of what she was doing,
only knowing she had to get away.

She pulled out a second later, without looking

into her mirror to see if any other car was behind her. There was a scream of tyres, the blare of a horn, and another car skidded to a halt, almost colliding with the silver limousine as it slewed sideways to avoid Chloe's car.

'You stupid bitch!' The driver of the other car leaned out of his window, yelling hoarsely. 'You could have killed us both! Don't you use your bloody mirror?'

Deeply flushed, Chloe backed up slightly. She couldn't drive away without scraping the other car's wing. Still bellowing, the driver behind her drove on down the road, making an insulting gesture as he passed her. Chloe's head was bent, she only saw it out of the corner of her eye and she made no reply, an apology would only make matters worse, her scalded face and bent head were admission enough.

She hadn't looked towards the limousine, she didn't want to see Ben's face again. He must have seen the whole incident. The last thing Chloe wanted now was to meet his eyes. Her engine was still running, she put her hands on the wheel, shooting a quick look towards her wing mirror to make sure no other car was in sight. The road was clear, but before she could pull out again a hand came through her open window and she numbly watched as the long brown fingers switched off the ignition and withdrew the key.

Chloe looked up, startled, wide-eyed.

'Get out.' Ben spoke through tight lips, his long body bent to speak to her. Behind him Chloe saw the gleaming limousine sliding away.

A face showed at the rear side window briefly then the car put on speed and was gone.

'I . . .' She tried to speak and her throat closed up, she was shaking too much to be able to talk.

'If you try to drive now, you'll cause a real accident,' Ben told her coldly. He opened her door and leaned over to unhitch her seat belt. She shrank back in her seat at the sudden proximity of his body and felt his blue eyes stabbing at her, then the belt was released and slithered back. Ben took hold of her arm in an iron grip and pulled her out of the seat.

Straightening, she looked up at him, breathless with panic and resentment at the way he was manhandling her. 'Don't push me around like that!' The words came out unevenly and that made her angrier, she wanted to be cool and collected. When she was around Ben she always had trouble being cool and collected, that was what bothered her. She had always been able to stand back from everyone else, be in control of herself and whatever situation she faced, but Ben did something to her that wrecked her concept of herself, forced her to question her own attitudes, and that was frightening.

Still holding her with one hand, he deftly wound up the car window, slammed the door, locked it and tossed her the car keys before he began to walk back towards his house, taking her with him in spite of her struggle to release herself.

'What do you think you're doing?' Chloe demanded, almost forgetting that she had come here to apologise to him. One look at him and she had begun to regret her impulsive decision to see him again. Ben was no longer approachable; there was no point in telling him that she knew Jilly had lied. He wouldn't care whether she knew the truth or not.

'You need a drink.'

'I don't want one. I'm in a hurry, I haven't got time. Let go!' she muttered the last words as he hustled her into the hall. It hadn't changed, even if its owner had—her glance moved over everything, recognising it, the dark blues and reds of the carpet, the smooth gloss of the cream walls, the deep polished gleam of some hall chairs and the mahogany table on which stood a round stone bowl of spring flowers, their perfume fresh and disturbing; oddly nostalgic.

Ben released her and shut the front door. A woman in a neat black dress hovered, watching them as if uncertain what she should do. Ben came up behind Chloe and she stiffened as she felt his hands on her shoulders, then he pulled her coat off and tossed it to the woman who had moved to take it, her sloe-eyed gaze on Chloe's flushed face. Ben transferred his hand to Chloe's elbow and under the other woman's curious stare Chloe wasn't going to protest again, she walked beside Ben into the room whose windows looked out into the street.

The door closed and Ben moved towards some decanters on a table against the wall. 'Sit down,' he said curtly, picking up a glass.

Chloe slowly walked towards a deep, stone-

coloured couch, realising that he had had this
room re-decorated since she was last here. It was
more muted, the colours calm and restrained, the
walls papered in a smooth silky pink so delicate
that it seemed to be a white which was coloured
by a rose light shining on it. On one wall hung a
large, dark Elizabethan portrait of a woman in a
ruff and a plum-coloured gown—she stared out
of the canvas with an arrogance so sure of itself
that it did not even need to be assertive. Her eyes
held you at bay. A very old grandfather clock
stood in one corner and that Chloe did
remember; its case was heavily gilded with scenes
of country life.

As she sat down, Ben came over to her with a
glass, holding it out. 'A small brandy,' he said as
she took it reluctantly. 'You almost had a nasty
accident out there.' He had another glass in his
left hand. He sat down with it on the corner of
the couch, leaving a gap between himself and
Chloe.

She stared into the glass, moistening her lips
with the tip of her tongue in a nervous way, then
caught her inner lip between her teeth. How
could she start? The words wouldn't come. She
vaguely knew how Jilly had felt earlier; guilt was
like a padlock on the tongue.

'What were you doing out there?' Ben
suddenly asked, and she took a deep breath.

'I wanted to see you. To tell you . . .' Her
mind was in such confusion that she stopped
again, swallowing. Her fingertips were so tightly
clasped around the glass that she could see the

whorled white pads of them through the amber
liquid.

'What?' he demanded impatiently, and the
sharp tone precipitated her into speech.

'Jilly admitted she lied.' It was out at last and
she felt herself slacken in relief, as though merely
saying that made it easier to go on, but before she
could say any more, apologise, tell him how badly
she felt about having believed her niece instead of
him, Ben laughed harshly.

'What took her so long?'

Chloe couldn't look at him, she began to
babble huskily. 'I can't tell you how sorry I am—
you have every right to be angry . . .'

'Thank you.' His succinct remark interrupted
the flow and she looked at him helplessly, looking
away at once, appalled by the grimness of his
face.

'That's why I am here—I came without
thinking, Jilly only just admitted the truth to
me, I was horrified, I had to apologise, I
wanted you to know that we all knew Jilly had
lied, I feel dreadful about what happened.' She
stopped talking, looking down. What had she
expected? Ben was coldly angry and nothing she
was saying would soften the way he felt. Ben
had always known himself to be innocent, her
news was no surprise to him, and why had she
ever thought he would care whether his name
had been cleared as far as she and her family
were concerned?

'Drink your brandy,' he said and she obeyed
without thinking because it gave her something to

do. All she wanted was to get away from that hard, icy face and those distant, hostile eyes.

Ben lifted his own glass and swallowed his brandy, then put down the empty glass on a table nearby. The tiny clink made Chloe jump, she clutched at her own half-empty glass, her throat heated by the brandy. She drank some more and felt slightly better.

'I realise an apology isn't much use at this late stage but I felt I had to offer it to you, for Jilly as much as for myself and my family. I thought you had a right to know that we all knew the truth.' Jilly would have told her mother, of course, she would have known that if *she* didn't, Chloe would. Dorry was going to be in quite a state, Chloe felt sorry for her sister. It would be even more of a shock to Dorry and Clive, they were more deeply involved with Jilly; finding out that she had lied to them about something so serious would distress them and make them question their whole relationship with their daughter. Chloe felt that Jilly had made a fool of *her*—how would Jilly's parents feel?

She was nursing her empty glass, her head still lowered. Ben moved and she nervously glanced sideways out of the corner of her eye, tension crackling at her nerve-ends. He took the glass from her and slammed it down on the table next to his, the silence in the room like an electric fence between them—sparks from it filled the air with blue flashes.

'What do you expect me to say?' he asked

through his teeth, his mouth curling in a faint sneer. 'That all is forgiven and forgotten? Well, too bad—because I don't feel inclined to do either. Three years ago your niece accused me of attacking her . . .'

'No, she didn't say that!' protested Chloe.

'Put it how you like,' he brushed her protest aside. 'She accused me of something I didn't do. You didn't ask me if I'd done what she claimed. You didn't even query a word of what she said, you simply condemned me without a hearing. I stood there and waited for you to look at me and ask: did you? But you didn't doubt her word for a second, did you? You'd made up your mind I was guilty before I even arrived. I walked into that room and you looked at me as if you hated me.' He stood up and she shrank back on the couch, breathless with panic as she saw the anger leaping in his eyes. 'And nothing has changed, has it? You've just told me that Jilly lied and now you know it, but you haven't asked me a single question. You're still accepting everything she says—what I have to say doesn't matter. Your apology is meaningless. God knows why you bothered to come.'

She shifted as if she was going to say something and he leaned towards her, his lean body rigid with a savagery that belied the civilised formality of the immaculately tailored dark grey suit he wore. His anger was out of place in those clothes, in this serenely elegant room. He vibrated with a feeling that ate at her nerves; three years ago her eyes had accused and hated him and now the tables were turned and Ben's eyes made her want to run away.

'I always knew I was innocent,' he said bitingly. 'I don't need you to tell me and you can't wipe out what happened with a polite apology.'

'I'm sorry,' she muttered, getting up, and stumbled because the shocks she had had over the past couple of hours, combined with the brandy, had made her light-headed.

Ben steadied her instinctively, a hand at her waist, and she looked up at him. The glossy black hair she remembered so well was touched here and there with a streak of silver, she suddenly saw. The blue eyes which had once been so vital and full of warmth when they looked at her had become ice-floes in the austere regions of his face, when her glance collided with them she felt herself sink helplessly, and shivered. This was not the man she had loved—that casual, lithe man whose fierce energy had been softened by tenderness when he smiled at her. This was a distant stranger who did not like her.

'I am sorry, Ben,' she whispered.

'So you said.' He was still very close but although he was physically mere inches away, he couldn't have been further if there had been the whole world between them. Chloe felt diminished, stricken, she couldn't blame him for his anger but she shivered in the face of it.

'I thought I knew Jilly so well,' she said. 'It didn't occur to me that she could have invented the whole thing, I'd known her all her life and she had never done anything like that before. Jilly may exaggerate, even stretch the truth at times, but she had never actually lied before. How could I take your side against my own niece?'

'No reason,' he said with that hostile mouth. 'Except possibly that you had told me you loved me.'

All the blood left her face; the words were aimed like a stiletto, she felt them pierce her skin and trembled violently, looking down, her lashes a dark fringe against the stretched white skin of her upper cheekbones.

'But it seems your family have a habit of using words without meaning them,' Ben added deliberately, as if he enjoyed hurting her.

She couldn't answer that, there was nothing she could say in her own defence, the only thing she could do was go before he hurt her even more. The elegant room echoed with the harshness of the feeling between them; her nerves were scraped raw by it. Yet what had she expected? She had hurt Ben badly three years ago; was it surprising that he wanted his revenge? Those accusations had been insult enough—it must have made it far worse that she believed him guilty without so much as asking him one question. What good had it done to come here to apologise and explain? Ben was right. God knows why she had bothered.

'I don't know why you've come here,' he said as if he had read her mind.

'I felt I had to,' she managed to whisper. 'I owed it to you.' She even owed him this contemptuous assault; Ben had a right to be angry with her. He couldn't be more scornful of her than she was herself; she might rationalise with hindsight and tell herself that she had believed him guilty because she was jealous and afraid, because she half expected him to leave her, stop wanting her, but the bitter fact was that she had not doubted Jilly's story and it had been a lie. Ben was not angry with Jilly. He was angry with Chloe. The violence of his anger was a measure of how much he had cared in the first place, and she wanted to cry as that dawned on her. She had been terrified that Ben would one day tire of her, but she had ended their love herself.

'I'd better go,' she said, giving him a brief look, her lashes fluttering upwards and the dark centres of her eyes enormous, lustrous with feeling.

Ben stared down into them, his face taut. His lips were pressed tightly together, his nostrils flared, he was breathing harshly. Anger still hardened his face but in that quick look Chloe saw something else; Ben was controlling other emotions, his eyes had a deep heat which made her body stiffen.

'You're thinner,' he said abruptly.

'Am I? I suppose I am.' She answered automatically but she wasn't thinking about what either of them was saying, she was wondering what that look in his eyes meant, and fighting against an intense excitement she was afraid to feel.

'Still singing?'

'Yes.' Her mouth shaped the word, her mind was busy with other things. 'I saw you on television this morning,' she said and it seemed so long ago—not hours but days. So much had happened since, her mind reeled with the shock of realising that it had only been that morning that she and Jilly had seen him. She had been so concerned for Jilly, so worried in case seeing Ben had ruined her wedding day. The bitter irony of it made her laugh but it was more a contraction of the face in pain than amusement and Ben stared down at her, his brows ragged.

'What's funny?' he asked in biting impatience and nothing was, she shook with misery, moving away.

'Nothing. Nothing at all.' It would be a long time before she found anything to smile about. 'I must go. I'm sorry, I know it's useless saying it but what else can I say?' There were really no words to meet this situation; she had wronged Ben too deeply.

She was at the door. He hadn't spoken and she didn't wait to see if he would, she went out, wondering what the woman had done with her coat, but she didn't have to look around for it because the next second the woman was there, offering the shabby old coat with a neutral expression which was so careful not to comment on the garment that it was quite comment enough.

'Thank you.' Chloe turned to let the woman put it on, and saw Ben in the doorway.

'Goodbye,' she said in his direction and hurried to the front door. She hadn't said goodbye three years ago. He had just gone and she had been silent. Now she was going and he was silent; as if they were going through the movements of some slow, strange dance, echoing each other. She almost jumped as she felt the front door slam. She got into her car and drove away and all the time she was wondering if Ben would watch her from the windows of the room she had just left, but if he did she caught no glimpse of him, no curtain stirred, no face swam dimly in the recesses of the room. It was over, but then she had thought it was over for the last three years, she hadn't expected to see Ben again, she had said her goodbye inside herself as he walked out of her sister's house, that terrible day. She couldn't have imagined then that three years later she would see that whole situation in reverse; time held odd surprises.

Why had his eyes watched her with that strange deep inner glow? Her mouth was dry, she shuddered as she remembered that look. Anger, she told herself—that was what it must have been, of course. One emotion can look much like another if it is fierce enough. Ben's eyes had burnt with anger and she was crazy if she let herself wonder if that passionate glow had been anything else.

She drove back to her flat which was a two minute walk from the Tate Gallery, in a back street of Victorian houses which were too large for a modern family and had been converted into flats which still had a certain style and spacious airiness. Chloe had a five year lease and had decorated the three rooms in her own taste. It was a pleasant enough environment, but she didn't suffer from home-sickness if she had to be away from it for weeks on end when she did a job elsewhere, abroad or in another part of the country. The flat felt temporary, she hadn't spent much on the modern furniture, there was nothing in the place she cared about, except a rosewood sofa table made in 1801 which had belonged to her great-grandmother, a desk she had picked up in a junk shop, and her own collection of books, records and tapes. She had potted plants arranged everywhere, it added a little reality to the rooms, but that apart the flat was just a dormitory for her body. Her mind was always elsewhere.

If she looked out of the window she could see at the end of the street the distant, grey-blue, metallic glint of the river. Some mornings she went for a walk before the city woke up and stood for a long time watching the flow of the waters, down past Greenwich and the marshes to the open sea. She always felt wistful then; wishing she was floating with it, escaping with the river from the chains of the city which bound them both.

When she got back she made herself some coffee. She was just sitting down with a cup when the 'phone rang. It was Gil, sounding baffled.

'So where did you get to?' he demanded and

she was at a loss for words for a minute because
she had forgotten all about him.

'I'm sorry, Gil . . .'

'So I should think. What happened? It was the
bride who was meant to be going away, not you. I
hung around for an hour before I realised you
weren't coming back. I felt a real prawn.'

'Something happened,' she said.

'Well, obviously. Was it so earth-shattering
that you couldn't come and tell me you were
leaving?' Gil was irritable now, his voice grating.

'Yes,' she said simply because that was the
truth. 'I had a shock,' she said. 'But I'm sorry I
walked out on you like that, honestly. It was very
bad-mannered of me.'

Gil made a grumbling noise. 'Okay, I forgive
you—thousands wouldn't.' He paused. 'What
sort of shock? What happened?' he asked. 'Funny
you should say that, your sister seemed to be in
quite a state, too. I asked her where you had got
to and she stared at me as if she didn't know who
I was then gave a sort of wail and almost ran
away.'

Chloe could imagine. Poor Dorry. She gave a
sigh. 'I can't talk about it,' she said with a sense
of irony. She hadn't even been able to talk to
Ben; her mind was jammed with too many
painful images, how could she talk to an outsider
like Gil?

'I hate weddings, they depress me,' Gil said
irrelevantly, then she laughed because it was
really very relevant, wasn't it? What a day to
choose to tell her—Jilly was amazing! Yet when

one thought about it, had it been such an inexplicable occasion for such a confession? Jilly was just leaving on her honeymoon, she would be away for three weeks and out of reach of any serious recriminations. By the time she got back everyone would be over the first shock and Jilly had probably worked out that she couldn't choose a better time to tell them. Even in her decision to tell the truth at last, Jilly had been self-protective, careful to time it to her own advantage.

'What on earth is funny about that?' Gil asked, even more bewildered.

'Not a thing,' she admitted. 'I must go, Gil. I'll see you on Monday, okay?'

'Rehearsals eleven o'clock,' Gil agreed. She was singing at the night-club where Gil worked most of the time. She had another fortnight of her current contract to run and then she planned to take a few weeks holiday before the summer season began and her work became more pressing. She was always busier in the summer. She hadn't had a summer holiday in years; she always took them out of season.

'You should have a good session with Annie,' Chloe told him. She herself wasn't working tonight, she had taken the evening off because she had intended to spend it with her family who were going on to a late supper after the wedding reception, but the club had managed to get a top jazz singer to fill in for her.

'Sure,' Gil said cheerfully. 'She's a great girl.'

When she had hung up, Chloe poured herself a

fresh cup of coffee and sat down to drink it while she watched the television news. It helped to keep her mind off the subject of Ben, but just as she was beginning to wind down the 'phone rang and she knew before she heard the voice at the other end that it was Dorry.

Her sister sounded as on edge as someone with a raging toothache. 'Where did you go?' she demanded and before Chloe answered, burst out: 'I can't believe Jilly would do this to me!'

'To *you*?' Chloe murmured but the irony was lost on Dorry.

'I couldn't believe it when she told me—how could she lie like that? I'll never sleep tonight. Jilly chose a fine time to tell me—when we were all so happy! She's ruined her own wedding day and I'd looked forward to it for so long, how could she do it to me? Clive isn't speaking to me. He seems to think it's all my fault. How could I guess that Jilly wasn't telling the truth? Who would have thought she'd lie like that? I said to him, why didn't *you* guess, then? Why is it my fault? He says he feels a fool, he says he damned near rang the police and then the fat would really have been in the fire. Wouldn't we have looked stupid if she came clean in a court full of strangers, thank God it never went further than the family.' Dorry drew a breath and Chloe thought she had finished, but then she burst out again. 'Can you believe it? I was knocked sideways. I've been ringing you for hours, we wondered what had happened to you, going off like that, of course you're upset, who wouldn't be, but why didn't you say you were leaving?'

'I went to see Ben Haskell,' Chloe said with bitterness because her sister had not so much as mentioned his name, she only saw the situation from her own angle.

Dorry had the decency to gulp. 'Oh, dear—did you? What did you say?'

'What do you think I said? Good heavens, Dorry, three years ago he was accused of interfering with a sixteen-year-old girl and today we found out it was all lies. Don't you think we owed him an apology?' She heard her sister make a sulky little noise.

'Of course, Clive has been telling me we had to do something, write to him or ... well, it's so difficult to know what to say. What's he going to do? He won't sue us for libel or something, will he? That's what I thought—I said to Clive, he could sue us for libel if we admit anything.'

'Dorry,' Chloe said on a harsh sigh. 'My God, Dorry ...' But what was the use of saying anything to her sister? Dorry was reacting with typical self-centred blindness to everything but her own interests. She was alarmed about the consequences of Jilly's confession but she was still trying to protect her daughter, as well as herself; she simply didn't see anything from anyone else's angle.

'Well, we aren't rich, you know—he is, he could afford a court case just to get his own back, he was very angry, and I know Jilly shouldn't have lied about him but she didn't mean it, she didn't want to cause all that trouble, she told me she was terribly upset.'

Chloe sighed again. 'Ben won't sue you for libel.' She paused then asked with conscious irony: 'Did Jilly get to the airport on time?' She was sure that nothing would have stopped her niece catching that plane—whoever had to pay for the past it wasn't going to be Jilly.

'Oh, yes,' Dorry said, unaware of her sister's tone. 'Clive drove them to the airport himself.'

'Well, she's Tony's problem now,' Chloe said. She didn't envy him his future, Jilly had been totally spoilt by her parents, particularly Dorry. 'I'm tired, Dorry, I'm going to get an early night,' she said.

'It isn't that late,' Dorry said, faintly sulky. She needed a wailing wall to tell her troubles to but Chloe refused to play the part. She had no one to confide in and she had enough troubles of her own.

'I'm sorry, I'm dead,' she said with flat finality and hung up, but she didn't go to bed, she sat up listening to music and brooding, hearing the sound high up inside her skull as she mentally sang with it; a mournful traditional blues song she had sung before, the wail of the clarinet like the sound of cats on city roofs at night. She played it over and over again; it exactly fitted her mood. It was easier than crying. Chloe wasn't the type that cried; she was the type that hated to show her feelings, was afraid of weakness, needed to be in control and felt a flare of panic when she sensed herself losing her grip on what was happening to her.

She slept very late on the Sunday morning, staggering out of bed around noon with a splitting headache and a queasy stomach. She skipped lunch and drank some ice-cold orange juice with two crisp-bread as a brunch, then went for a brisk walk to wake herself up. In the afternoon she drove out into the country, had tea at a small country hotel and drove back in the gathering dusk. She watched TV for an hour that evening and went to bed very early. This time she slept and woke on the Monday feeling more or less normal after a solid nine hours sleep.

She had a daily routine which she followed rigidly; habit made it easier to do her various exercises. She spent half an hour working out in a sleek black leotard which allowed her freedom of movement, then she did her vocal exercises. Both were essential—you had to be fit to sing. A healthy body produced a healthy voice, and she knew that her lungs could bring out a deeper note when she had spent some time in physical exercise beforehand.

At eleven she was at the night-club, rehearsing with Gil. He was still curious about what had happened at the wedding reception to make her rush off like that, but she managed to fend off his questions. They worked for nearly two hours then Gil took her to lunch at a nearby restaurant which specialised in wholefood. Chloe had a fruit and nut salad but only ate half of it, she had no appetite today. Gil gave her a concerned stare as he finished his own large plate of Aubergine

Provencal, a rich dish melting with a cheese sauce over the finely sliced vegetables.

'You're looking very down. What *is* bothering you, Chloe?'

'I'm just not hungry, okay?'

'If you say so,' he muttered. 'But I don't buy that. Something is wrong—I wish you'd tell me, you have nasty black circles under your eyes, in case you hadn't noticed.'

'My voice is fine, that's all that matters,' she said stubbornly.

'You need more than a voice to make the people sit up and listen,' Gil said and he was right, of course—it was that extra punch that she normally produced that made her a popular singer.

'I'll have more,' she said, hoping she was right. 'Tonight. You'll see.'

Sometimes when she was emotionally disturbed it helped her music; the pain came out in her voice and dissolved in the air. Singing was a release, you expressed what you couldn't put into words and that charged your singing with more power than you normally possessed. She hoped that was how it would be tonight, but she couldn't tell Gil that, he would only ask more questions she didn't want to answer.

After lunch she drove back to her flat to rest for a few hours. That was another part of her routine. She worked at the night-club until quite late, she had learnt to spend some time recharging during the afternoon. You couldn't work flat out, you had to put back what you took out.

The club was crowded when she went on that night. The comedian had worked the audience up into noisy enjoyment with his act. He introduced her, walking backwards with an arm flung out as Chloe came on stage. She knew from the roars of laughter that he was pulling funny, mock-lustful faces behind her.

'Isn't she lovely? Now, don't all rush, I'm dating her tonight, you've lost your chance but give her a big hand, Chloe Tyrrell, ladies and gentlemen.' He walked off clapping vigorously and Chloe flung him a smile sideways, getting back a cheerful wink. He did more or less the same patter every night and it always worked; he could hold the audience in the hollow of his hand. As she began to sing the wolf-whistles and stamping feet died down, the house lights dimmed, one blue spot focused on her at the microphone in the centre of the stage. Chloe swallowed nervously. It was stupid, she had been singing professionally for years, yet she still got the same sick spasms of terror every time she began. It passed off quickly enough but it was bad for a few seconds.

Her dress shimmered as she swayed, tiny sequins overlapping like the silver scales on a fish to give the dress a rippling, unbroken line. It clung everywhere it touched. Her shoulders and arms were bare, the bodice hugged her breasts tightly before curving in to her waist then fell glittering to her feet. 'You look like a mermaid,' Gil had said when he first saw it.

On stage she looked quite different, it was a

deliberate transformation from her everyday, cool look to this dazzling image. She had sprayed faint silvery glitter on her hair, which she styled herself in the dressing-room with electrically heated rollers just before going on; her lids had a sparkle of green shadow, her mouth had become glossy, sensual, a warm red curve, her skin was smooth, lucent, nacreous. The voice which swelled up into the smoky air was surprising, too; Chloe's range was enormous and the sound she could produce had a full, rich firmness, a sureness she worked for daily with those endless, repeated exercises.

She was halfway through her act when she saw a man sitting at a table on her right, leaning back in his chair with his face out of the circle of pink light from the fringed lamp on his table. Chloe stiffened as her eye touched him. For one minute she couldn't believe it; she thought she must be seeing things, but then he shifted in his chair and she was certain she recognised him. He was alone, a glass of champagne on the table by his hand, his formal evening clothes and dignified air making him an odd member of their usual audience. What was Ben Haskell's father doing here?

CHAPTER THREE

'WHAT the hell is wrong with you?' Gil demanded, following her off stage at the end of her act. 'I've never heard you sing so badly.'

The audience was still applauding noisily and Chloe glanced back over her shoulder at the lighted area, her face quizzical. 'They don't seem to think so.'

'What do they know?' Gil retorted. 'You hit the right notes and made a nice noise, that's all they care about—and you look pretty sexy in that dress, you sparkle like the fairy on the Christmas tree. Of course they like you. But that doesn't mean you sang as well as you can sing, now does it?'

She walked into her dressing-room, grimacing. 'Okay, I sang badly tonight. I'm sorry. I've got something on my mind.'

'What?' Gil asked, standing in the doorway impatiently, watching her as she put a hand to her zip. 'I'll do that,' he added and deftly unzipped the dress, watching Chloe wriggling out of it. She hung it on a hanger and slipped a cotton wrapper on, then turned and gave Gil an apologetic smile.

'It's personal.'

'Look, Chloe, you're supposed to be a professional. If it's personal, keep it out of your working life. When you're on stage you should forget everything but what you're out there to do, you know that.'

'Sorry,' she said shortly and Gil gave her a quick, searching look.

'And don't sulk.' He grinned and went out, closing the door. Chloe sat down at the dressing-table. She would be going on again in an hour, the cabaret was split into two halves because the audience changed during the evening. Clients drifted in and out again, few people stayed for more than a couple of hours. They went on to other clubs or went home and a new influx would be sitting out there when she went out to do her second spot. She never sat around in her stage costumes, they creased if you sat down in them. They weren't meant for ordinary wear. The silver one wasn't even meant for walking; it was so tight that she had to take tiny steps very slowly. From out front it might look as if she was gliding gracefully—or that was what she hoped! But she knew that she was merely concentrating on each step so that she didn't split her skirt.

She carefully dusted her make-up to take off the shine which heat and nervous excitement had given her skin. Her hand shook, she was very nervous, tense with anticipation, although she wasn't sure what it was that she expected. Ben Haskell's father wasn't the type to visit night-clubs alone so what was he doing here tonight? She was certain he must have come here to see her, but why? She had never met him when she was seeing Ben. Had Ben sent him here?

She heard the knock on the door without surprise. Stiffening, she stared into the mirror. 'Yes?'

The door opened slowly. His eyes met hers in the mirror as he walked forward. 'May I come in, Miss Tyrrell?'

'You seem to be in,' Chloe said as she watched him close the door without waiting for her answer. She wasn't good at guessing ages, especially where men were concerned, but she was sure Mr Haskell must be seventy, at least. He moved stiffly, his shoulders bent, his face lined with more than age—she sensed that pain had written some of those lines. He had that indefinable weariness that sometimes comes with a long illness.

She stood up, the cotton robe rippling over her thighs, and held out a hand. 'How do you do? It's Mr Haskell, isn't it?'

'Joseph Haskell,' he expanded, shaking her hand. His fingers were dry and cool, she felt the swollen knuckles and bowed fingers. He had arthritic hands, the skin wrinkled and blue. 'You recognised me?' he asked, smiling.

'I've seen a photograph of you.'

'Ah, yes,' he said, his face clearing. 'Ben has several in his sitting room, doesn't he?'

Chloe didn't answer that. 'Please, sit down,' she said because he looked so frail that she was afraid it tired him to stand, and watched the care with which he moved to a chair, the slow way he sat down, the relief in his face as he did so.

Chloe sat down again on her dressing-table

stool, arranging the robe across her knees with one hand.

'I enjoyed your performance very much,' he said. 'I'm a jazz fan, did my son tell you that?'

Chloe's eyes opened wide. 'No, he didn't.'

'Well, I am—I started listening to good jazz forty years ago, the first time I ever visited the States. I was managing a hotel in Los Angeles for two years. The first year I was there we had some jazz musicians staying with us. They invited me to go down to New Orleans to stay with them for a week. I went and I heard bands that blew my mind.' He grinned at her, the weary dignity of his face breaking up in lines of wicked amusement at her visible surprise. 'Nothing I've heard since has been that good but I still collect jazz recordings. I have a huge collection, you must hear some of it sometime.'

Chloe was too taken aback to answer; Ben had never mentioned his father's passion for jazz but then Ben had never talked much about his family. He was in some ways a secretive man, there were whole areas of his life she knew nothing about.

'I'm seventy years old next week,' Mr Haskell told her suddenly.

'Congratulations,' she smiled.

'I'm going to have a big party at my house on the river, just past Henley, there will be over a hundred guests.'

'That should be fun, I hope you enjoy it.' Chloe was still at sea—why was he here and why was he telling her about his birthday party? She had been expecting him to talk about Ben, but he hadn't done more than mention him in passing. It was baffling.

'I'll enjoy it far more if you'll come along and sing for us,' he said and the shock made her sit up, her eyes startled.

'Me? Sing at your party?' She was babbling, trying to think, to work out exactly what this invitation meant. She stared at him intently, searching his face. 'Did Ben suggest . . .'

'No, Ben doesn't know anything about it,' Mr Haskell said and Chloe flushed.

'Oh, I see. Well, I'm flattered, of course, but . . .'

'Miss Tyrrell, I'm a very old man and I doubt if I'll have much longer to live.' His shoulders stooped again, his face had a melancholy droop to it, his voice was quietly sad—Chloe was stricken by the way he looked at her, the reproach and pleading in his eyes, until she suddenly felt a qualm of doubt as he went on talking. 'You wouldn't refuse an old man a last few hours of pleasure, would you?'

She eyed him thoughtfully. He was acting and as their eyes met she saw the flicker of laughter in his face.

'That was a disgraceful piece of blackmail,' she said, but couldn't help smiling back at him.

'Well, it was worth trying,' he said, unabashed. 'You see, I want you at my party, Miss Tyrrell—won't you come?'

'Why do you want me there?' she asked guardedly, unsure how much he knew.

He put both hands on his knees and studied the

polished caps of his shoes. 'Ben means a great deal to me. He's never been one to talk about his private life but I've learnt how to make a good guess at what is going on inside his head. A few years ago he mentioned you to me a few times. He said he'd introduce us soon. I got the impression I was about to meet my future daughter-in-law.'

Chloe felt herself paling and looked down, knowing that he was watching her, and trying to conceal what she was feeling.

'And then suddenly he stopped talking about you. I didn't like to ask him what had gone wrong. He was short-tempered and difficult. Anyone who crossed him got his head bitten off. For a long time he worked with what I can only describe as desperation; he didn't have a private life, he didn't have time. Ben has always been a disciplined man. Two years ago he was more than that—he was obsessed with work. He was deliberately filling every waking hour with it. No human being can keep up that sort of drive for long. A year ago Ben caught a chill, didn't look after himself and ended up with pneumonia. He was forced to rest and that may well have saved his sanity, if not his life.'

Chloe laced her fingers to hide the tremor in them. What Ben's father was telling her made her hate herself. She had done that to Ben. No wonder he had looked at her with such bitterness on Saturday, she deserved it. He would never forgive her. She would never forgive herself; because all that Ben's father was telling her showed her so clearly how much Ben had cared for her. Ben had loved her and she had thrown his love back in his face.

'On doctor's orders he took a month's holiday in the Bahamas. When he came back he seemed normal enough—on the surface. He works hard but he doesn't push himself to the limit any more. All the same, he isn't happy.'

Chloe turned her head away to hide the expression in her face, but she was afraid she wasn't hiding anything from the old man watching her so intently. Ben's father was a sharp old man. Ben might not have told him anything—but Mr Haskell was making some very shrewd guesses.

'I'd almost forgotten all about you until I saw you outside Ben's house the other day,' Mr Haskell said gently. 'Ben was talking. He stopped suddenly and I saw he had gone a funny shade of white. I thought for a second that he was ill. I said something and he didn't hear a word. He looked like a man in acute shock. I looked in the direction he was staring and I saw you in that car, then you started to pull out and almost crashed into the other car. Ben walked away as if he didn't remember I was there.'

Chloe got up, shaking, her hands thrust into the pockets of her robe. She stood with her back to Mr Haskell, her head bent.

'This is none of my business. I'm not involved with your son. You shouldn't be telling me all this.'

'Ben isn't happy,' Mr Haskell said very quietly.

Chloe bit her lip. 'I'm very sorry, but there's nothing I can do to help him, I wish there was.'

'You can sing at my party.'

She laughed harshly. 'You've got it all wrong, Mr Haskell—you seem to think that Ben wants to see me. He doesn't. He hates me. If I sang at your party, he would ignore me or walk out. I hurt his feelings three years ago and he hasn't forgiven me; he told me he never will.'

'That doesn't sound like indifference,' Mr Haskell said slowly. 'It sounds like wounded pride and Ben has plenty of pride. He's quite capable of cutting off his nose to spite his face. Surely you aren't that silly, Miss Tyrrell?'

She gave a little sigh. 'No, Mr Haskell, but what can I do? I can hardly chase after him when he walks away from me, can I?'

'Why not? Isn't this the era of the liberated woman? If I'm right and Ben still cares for you, wouldn't it be stupid to let his pride stand in your way?'

Chloe stared at him, dumbfounded, and he smiled at her, his pale blue eyes bright and mischievous.

'Stand up for women's rights,' he said teasingly. 'If you want the man, go and get him.'

Chloe laughed helplessly, shaking her head. 'It isn't that simple.'

The stage manager rapped at her door. 'On in five minutes, Miss Tyrrell.'

'Okay, Pete,' she said automatically. Smiling at Mr Haskell she said: 'I'm sorry, I'm afraid you have to leave now—I must get dressed for my second show.'

'Of course,' he said, moving slowly to the door. With one hand on the handle, he turned to look at her. 'Please come and sing at my party, Miss Tyrrell.' He pulled a printed card out of his jacket and handed it to her. 'There's my address. The party is on Sunday evening; you can sing at any time you choose. Bring your pianist, or would you like me to arrange that?'

She held the card, turning it over between her fingers. 'No, if I come I'll bring Gil.' She looked up and smiled a little sadly at him. 'It was a pleasure to meet you, Mr Haskell.'

'We'll meet again,' he said, opening the door. 'You aren't going to be as stubborn and unbending as my son, Chloe. May I call you Chloe? It's a beautiful name and it belongs to a beautiful girl.' The door closed and he was gone; she stared at the card, her face a battleground.

Over the next few days she continually argued with herself; torn between the wish to see Ben again and a realisation of how humiliating it would be if he ignored her. Ben had loved her once, but now he despised and disliked her—those icy, forbidding eyes had told her so last time they met. Only a masochist would deliberately go out of her way to give him another chance to stare at her with that chilling distaste. Yet she couldn't forget what his father had told her; his description of Ben's unhappiness since they split up. Was he right in thinking that Ben still cared for her? That doesn't sound like indifference, he had said, and he was right—but did it sound like love? Chloe had seen no love in Ben's eyes—unless that odd smouldering insistence she had briefly glimpsed had been the last flickering ember of the love Ben had once felt?

She stared at herself in her dressing-room mirror the Friday following Mr Haskell's visit. What did you do when a fire was going out? Blow on the embers, she told herself, grimacing at her own reflection.

'Having fun?'

She jumped at the voice and met Gil's eyes in the mirror. 'What?'

'You were pulling horrible faces at yourself,' he said, lounging against the door. 'What are you trying to do? Frighten yourself into going on stage? You haven't really been with it all week. Pull yourself together.'

'Sorry, Gil. I'm tired, I suppose. I'm nearly at the end of this contract and I need a holiday.'

'That's no excuse for a bad performance. It isn't like you, Chloe. You've lost all your fire—get the bellows working.'

She stared at him in the mirror, transfixed.

'What's wrong now?' he asked, amused. 'You could drive a truck into your mouth. What did I say to make your jaw drop?'

It seemed so odd that Gil had picked up her own metaphor and used it in another context. Chloe made up her mind suddenly, at that second. 'Are you doing anything on Sunday?' she asked and Gil looked amused.

'Not that I can remember—why, are you inviting me out?'

'I've been asked to sing at a party—would you play for me?'

'Oh, work,' he said, disgusted.

She laughed. 'Afraid so.'

'What sort of party is it?'

'I've no idea. Do you know the Luxor Hotel chain? They own the new hotel on the edge of Hyde Park—the one with the twin silvery towers.'

Gil nodded. 'Is that where the party is?'

'No, the man who founded the Luxor hotels is giving the party—Joseph Haskell, he's seventy this week and this is his birthday party. He's a big jazz fan. I don't know if anyone else will be playing there but he's asked me to sing.'

Gil pursed his lips in a whistle. 'What's the fee?'

Chloe stared, taken aback.

Gil's brows lifted slowly, his face expressed incredulity. 'He didn't offer a fee? You didn't think of asking for one? Chloe, what is happening to you? You simply aren't in the same world as everyone else these days. You aren't in love, are you?'

She felt hot colour creeping up her face and Gil watched, his eyes becoming amused.

'This was a personal invitation,' she said crossly. 'To the party, I mean. It didn't enter my head to ask for a fee. Mr Haskell asked me himself.'

'Okay, don't get agitated about it. Well, I'm

not doing anything so I might as well come along
and see how the rich live. Where is this party?'

Chloe told him and Gil looked interested. 'I
don't know that side of London too well—it
could be a nice drive. Why don't you come in my
car? There's no point in both of us taking cars.
I'll pick you up at your flat in the evening. What
time?'

'Around seven-thirty?' she said with a feeling
of having burnt her bridges behind her.

'Okay,' Gil said. 'Now, put some power behind
your singing tonight, for God's sake. It isn't fair
to the audience to give them that lacklustre
performance. Let's end on a high, shall we?'

She smiled wryly at him. 'I'll give it everything
I've got.'

Gil relaxed, giving her a mock leer. 'And that's
plenty, baby.' He went, grinning, and Chloe
looked at herself in angry dismissal. Her skin had
a tired pallor, her eyes were faintly rimmed with
red, she showed the lack of sleep which was
making her on edge and irritable. At this moment
she didn't think she had anything to give anyone;
she was drained, exhausted. But she would find
the extra adrenalin Gil was demanding—somehow
between now and the moment when she walked
on stage she would dredge it up from her depths,
even if it meant another sleepless night and even
more weariness tomorrow. She was grateful to
Gil for nagging her, keeping her eyes on their
mutual goal. She depised herself because she was
letting her personal problems wreck her perform-
ances but she was giving too much of her energy

to her private life, there was little left at the end
of the day. She frowned angrily. There ought to
be—she was whining like a child, complaining
because life wasn't as easy as she would like it to
be, but Gil was right. She had no excuse for
singing badly. People paid to come and hear her;
they had a right to a good performance. It was
one of the laws of show business; a cliche,
mouthed all the time. The show must go on—
even if you're dead tired, miserable, in pain,
wanting only to crawl off and die. The show had
to go on. She shouldn't need to have that pointed
out to her by Gil.

She hadn't seen anything of her sister since the
wedding day; Dorry was sulking. Chloe knew
that without needing to see her, she had failed
Dorry and wouldn't be forgiven until Dorry
forgot all about it and she wouldn't do that until
Jilly got back from her honeymoon. Their mother
was in a cross mood too; she was waiting for her
granddaughter to return so that she could tell
Jilly what she thought of her. Hetty was furious
for having been made a fool of by the girl; she
had wasted pity on Jilly and it had all been a lie,
and now Hetty was fidgeting like a cat on hot
bricks waiting for a chance to let off steam. She
had called round to see Chloe several times to let
off some steam at her. One look at her mother
and Chloe had known she was boiling with fury.
For half an hour she couldn't get a word in
edgeways; Hetty scolded and complained, said
how amazed she was, predicted that Jilly would

be for it when she got back, her father was beside
himself, her mother was so angry she might do
anything, Hetty wanted to have a few words with
that young madam, a good slap that was what she
should have had but of course Dorry was too soft
with her. Always had been, a pity there hadn't
been any more babies, Dorry was one of those
women who were born to be mothers, she had no
more sense than a two-year-old. She had given
her life to Jilly and what had Jilly done in return?
Family life was a jungle; people preyed on each
other.

'If I had my turn again, I wouldn't marry and I
certainly wouldn't have children,' said Hetty.

'Thank you, Mother,' Chloe said ironically and
her mother glared at her.

'Don't be saucy with me, you know what I
mean. Trouble, nothing but trouble, that's what
children are, from the day they open their eyes.
Dorry should be grateful she only had one—you'd
think she'd have learnt her lesson by now, but
she'll make the same mistake again with Jilly's
children. It will be Dorry who gets left with
them, you can bet on that. Jilly will have her
baby-sitting morning, noon and night, and Dorry
will love it, more fool her.'

'If it makes them both happy,' Chloe began
and her mother laughed angrily.

'Jilly's selfish; that's Dorry's fault. That poor
man, what must he have felt like? Knowing he
hadn't done it but not able to prove Jilly was
lying? If I saw him again I wouldn't be able to
look him in the face.' Hetty stared at her

daughter searchingly. 'What did he say when you told him?'

'Very little. He's still angry and who can blame him?' Chloe's voice was stiff. She didn't want to talk about Ben, especially to one of her family—even if Ben could forgive her how could he ever forget what her family had done to him? He wouldn't want to see Jilly or her parents but Chloe's whole life had been spent in the same ambit, her family had always been an important part of her world. She refused to think about the choice she might be forced to make if she did persuade Ben to forgive her; it was too intolerable a prospect. The only thing more intolerable was the idea of turning down a chance of getting Ben back; the chance was so remote at this point that she could afford to put off thinking about what would happen if he did forgive her. There would be time enough for that later.

'I thought I might write to him,' Hetty said and Chloe was startled.

'Oh,' she gasped, not having expected it.

'What do you think? Should I? Dorry won't, she's scared that he might come back with a claim for damage to his reputation, but I think someone should—we owe the poor man an apology.'

Chloe didn't know what to say, but her mother wasn't so much asking her advice as thinking aloud. She talked for a minute about what she would say, then nodded in a satisfied way.

'Yes, I think I should, it's the decent thing to do—it should be Clive, of course, but Dorry won't let him and Clive is so embarrassed, he doesn't know what to say. Clive's so self-conscious about things like that; shyness, Dorry calls it but it's another sort of selfishness, I've always thought. Clive's more worried about what people will think of him than of how other people feel about themselves.'

Hetty was shrewd and clear-sighted about other people; she was full of restless energy even now in her old age. She couldn't resist arranging everyone's life for them. Ever since she arrived at Chloe's flat she had been up and down like a jack in the box, straightening a picture here, moving a vase there, darting about with one eye on her daughter and the other on the room they sat in; which was not arranged the way Hetty would have it if she lived here.

'Yes, I'll write to him,' she said as she left and Chloe had known that it would be useless to ask her not to do anything of the kind. Her mother wouldn't have listened. It gave Chloe nightmares to wonder what Ben would make of that letter; would he reply? Or just ignore Hetty's apology? So much of Chloe was bound up with her mother, so much of her concerned with Ben—she ached with uneasiness. She wouldn't blame Ben if he ignored the letter, yet she would be angry if he upset Hetty. It was all too perplexing, too complicated. She couldn't sleep for worrying about it.

On the Saturday morning Chloe rang the number on Mr Haskell's card but he was out. The woman who answered the 'phone took a message; Chloe *would* sing at the party and would be arriving between eight and nine.

While she was doing her housework that afternoon, Hetty arrived looking as if she might be going to explode any minute. Chloe eyed her warily as her mother sat down then jumped up again to plump up the cushions in the armchair she had chosen. While she was up she opened her handbag and produced a letter. 'Read this,' she ordered but as Chloe reluctantly took it, told her what it said in a furious voice. 'He thanks me for my letter but has no comment to make. Just that. Not a word more. Well! I don't know why he bothered to reply if that was all he had to say. I know he got a rough deal from Jilly—but he might at least have accepted my apology in the spirit in which I made it. Very rude, that's what I call it. Read it, read it—and you'll see what I mean.'

She sat down and Chloe looked over the letter; it was just two lines, she could read it in a glance and as her mother had told her what it said there wasn't much point, but Ben's anger breathed in every stiff, cold word.

She folded it again and gave it back to Hetty who crumpled it up and threw it into the fireplace. Chloe retrieved it wordlessly and dropped it into the wastepaper basket she kept under the writing desk near the window. It was a tiny piece of furniture, more ornamental than useful, she had bought it in a junk shop and had spent a lot of time restoring it to its original beauty. The gloss had gone from the rosewood when she found it, there had been chips in the slender legs. She had polished and repaired it and she loved it, useless though it was; she enjoyed seeing the sunlight playing over the delicately grained wood.

'What do you say to that?' her mother asked her and Chloe shrugged.

'What can I say? Did you really expect him to forgive and forget that easily?' The letter hadn't surprised her, it had been more or less what she expected.

'I wrote him a very nice letter,' Hetty said, aggrieved.

Chloe couldn't help smiling. 'I'm sorry, Mother.'

'Very rude,' Hetty said. 'Aren't you going to make some tea? I'd like a cup. Have you got any biscuits?' She was already on her way into the kitchen before she had finished talking. Chloe heard her filling the kettle. Sighing, Chloe wound the vacuum cleaner lead around the handle and stowed it away in the cupboard where she kept it. Hetty has just made the tea when someone rang the door bell. Chloe frowned, looking at her watch. Who could this be? Dorry? Had she got over her sulks?

'I'll take the tea in,' Hetty said as Chloe went to open the door. She passed, carrying a tray, looking back over her shoulder curiously to see who had arrived.

Chloe stared at Mr Haskell, dumbfounded to see him on her doorstep. 'I hope I'm not disturbing you when you're busy,' he said, smiling. 'I got your message and as I was passing this way I thought I'd call and ask you if your pianist would like to have some time rehearsing with the piano before the party started.'

'I'll get another cup,' Hetty said as easily as if she had known him for years. She had deposited her tray and come up behind Chloe who jumped at the sound of her mother's voice. Hetty took the opportunity of nipping past her daughter to offer her hand. 'I'm Chloe's mother, do call me Hetty,' she said with what Chloe could only describe as a flirtatious smile. Chloe winced; did her mother think she was eighteen?

'How do you? I am Joseph Haskell,' Ben's father said and Hetty did a very obvious double-take, staring at him. Chloe despairingly read the conflicting impulses in her mother's face as Hetty hovered between coldly walking away and satisfying her curiosity by drawing Mr Haskell into the house. Curiosity won. Hetty held on to his hand and urged him forward.

'We've just made some tea, you will have some, won't you? Chloe, get another cup.'

Chloe found the two of them seated on the couch together when she returned with the cup. Hetty had already poured tea for Mr Haskell who was nursing his cup and eating a digestive biscuit while he listened to Hetty's comments on the weather, the state of London traffic and the latest news.

'So you're Ben's father,' she murmured as Chloe poured herself some tea. 'Yes, I can see a resemblance. Did you say you were having a party?'

'A birthday party, I'm seventy tomorrow.'

'Seventy? Good heavens, you certainly don't look it—I thought you were years younger than me. Isn't it a blessing to keep your health? And you're having a birthday party—family all coming? Of course, quite an occasion. Seventy. Well, I am surprised. How old is your wife? I can't remember Ben mentioning his mother.'

'My wife died many years ago,' Mr Haskell said and Hetty looked sympathetic.

'Have some more biscuits,' she offered, moving closer. Chloe looked at her pointedly and Hetty ignored her. 'Ben isn't your only child, is he? He has sisters, is it two?'

'Yes, I had three children,' Mr Haskell said, taking another biscuit absent-mindedly.

'I had five,' Hetty said and he made noises of disbelief.

'Oh, yes—the eldest is forty now,' Hetty told him and he made even louder noises of disbelief. 'Dorry's over forty, in fact—my eldest daughter.'

'You don't look old enough to have a daughter that age,' Mr Haskell said, eying her admiringly.

'You're as young as you feel,' Hetty said and, judging by their present behaviour, neither of them felt a day over twenty. Chloe felt she was getting left out of the conversation; she coughed to remind them that she was in the room and her mother gave her a sweet smile.

'Darling, you aren't getting a cold, are you? Why don't you go and gargle with that marvellous stuff you use when you have a sore throat? You don't want to lose your voice.' She looked back at Mr Haskell. 'She has to be so careful.'

'I haven't got a sore throat, Mother,' Chloe said, putting an emphasis on the name.

'All the same, better not take risks, run along and gargle, there's a good girl.' From being a flirtatious teenager Hetty had rapidly become a commanding mother again; she fixed Chloe with a meaningful eye and Chloe reluctantly got up and left. What did Hetty think she was up to? Mr Haskell didn't seem to mind the way she was flirting with him, but Chloe minded. Her mother was almost seventy, when would she start acting her age? Chloe wouldn't have minded so much if Hetty had married one of the gentlemen who flocked around her, but her mother was enjoying herself too much. She said she didn't want to get tied down, marriage was a serious commitment and she wasn't ready to make it yet—she was having far too good a time as a single woman, and, anyway, a husband would interfere with her bridge.

Chloe went into the bathroom and looked down her throat. It was perfectly normal, of course, but she gargled a couple of times to satisfy Hetty. When she went back she found Mr Haskell on his feet.

'Oh, there you are, dear—I wondered where you had got to,' Hetty said maddeningly. 'I'm afraid I must be going, Mr Haskell is going to give me a lift home, isn't it kind of him?'

Chloe helplessly followed their progress to the door. Mr Haskell smiled at her as he ushered her mother out of the flat. 'So if your pianist wants to come early to try my piano, he's very welcome,' he said. 'I'm hoping to persuade your mother to come, too.'

Hetty extended an imperious hand. 'Chloe can bring me,' she said. 'I'll see you tomorrow, then, dear. Pick me up on your way. You can ring me and let me know what time you're leaving.'

Chloe stood, open-mouthed, watching them vanish. Her mother's lively voice floated up to her; Mr Haskell was laughing. Oh, dear, thought Chloe—I might have known Hetty would manage to complicate a situation which was already quite complex enough. God knows what she'll say to Ben tomorrow—she might say anything, she's as unpredictable as Dorry. Where had that streak of reckless mischief come from? It had been inherited by Jilly, but Chloe was grateful to have missed out on it, her common sense wouldn't let her act as erratically as the other women in her family.

I wonder if I could talk Mother out of going to the party? she thought, closing the door and walking back into her sitting room. Probably not, she admitted, sinking into a chair. Ben is going to be furious. It would have been bad enough for Chloe to be there; but how would he feel if his father danced attendance on Hetty all night the way he was doing now? Ben might be hostile to the Tyrrell family—but from the bemused way Mr Haskell had been watching Hetty he was very taken with her.

Oh, it's absurd, Chloe thought, fidgeting

restlessly in her chair. He's seventy and she isn't far behind him. How ridiculous to be worried about what they might get up—they aren't teenagers. Well, Mr Haskell wasn't. Chloe wasn't so sure about her mother.

She was even less sure on the Sunday evening when she and Gil stopped at Hetty's flat to pick her up. Hetty appeared in a very smart pale pink dress; she looked so young in it that Chloe did a double-take. It was cleverly chosen, she thought, fuming; that high, ruched lace neck which hid the wrinkled throat, those elegant tight sleeves which ended above the wrist to show off Hetty's small, delicate hands, the smooth lines of the dress which showed off her mother's slim figure. The dress was made of silk but had a lace over-gown and Hetty's tiny ears carried pink pearl drops which glowed against her silvery hair.

'I say,' Gil said admiringly. 'You look terrific, Mrs Tyrrell. A real charmer.'

Hetty inserted herself into the car, talking. 'What are you going to sing, Chloe? Not one of those dreadful shouting songs, I hope. Can't you sing something musical, for once? The sort of songs you sing at the night-club aren't at all suitable for a birthday party. That's a pretty dress, green suits you, brings out the colour of your eyes. The neckline's rather low, though. How long will it take to get there? Didn't you want to try the piano first, Gil? Mr Haskell said it had been tuned recently, so I suppose it will be all right, but I thought you would have liked to try it.'

'I hope I'll get a chance to do so before Chloe sings,' Gil said casually. 'As it is a party people aren't likely to notice if the piano isn't in tune; in my experience of parties nobody bothers to listen if anyone sings.' He grinned sideways at Chloe. 'Sorry, Chloe.' His eyes frowned concern as he noticed her face. 'You're looking pale—are you okay?'

'I'm fine,' she said quickly.

'You shouldn't have agreed to sing tonight, you've been working too hard,' Gil said with anxiety.

She leaned forward and switched on a tape of jazz which they had been listening to as they drove to pick up Hetty. 'Don't fuss,' she said. 'I want to hear that clarinet solo again; I can't believe how good he is.'

Hetty sat back in her seat and was blessedly quiet until they reached Joseph Haskell's house above the river a mile beyond Henley. It was a large white, gabled house set among pleasant gardens which ran down to the river bank. Chloe was intensely nervous as Gil turned in to the drive which was already full of cars. He dropped them at the front door and drove round to find somewhere to park. The door was opened by a small, grey-haired woman in a frilly white apron, but as they walked into the oak-panelled hall Joseph Haskell came out to meet them, his hands extended to take Hetty's.

'What an enchanting dress,' he said, gazing at her as if she was a dream come true. 'I didn't think they made dresses like that any more. I remember my mother had one very similar only it was floor length and had a bustle—or was it a train? I used to think she was so graceful in it, the back swayed as she walked.'

'I know what you mean,' Hetty said. 'Clothes were clothes in those days, not just something people threw on because they couldn't think what to wear.'

'I couldn't agree more. Sweat shirts . . . what an ugly name for an even uglier object! Even my own son wears those disgusting jeans at times— no style.'

'Oh, they don't know what the word means,' Hetty said, slipping her hand through his arm. 'You look very handsome in your evening clothes—I do like a man to dress with style. It makes a woman feel special.'

Chloe stood, glowering, waiting for Mr Haskell to notice her, wondering if she ought to go into the party without waiting for further invitation. She could hear laughter, music, voices and the clink of glasses. It was a very different sound to the usual party noise her friends made; these were very polite voices and no doubt they were drinking very different sorts of drink. No beer or vodka and tomato juice would be served here. Madeira? she wondered? Sherry? Or would they be daring and go for gin and tonic?

The house was furnished in a timeless English fashion with chintz and polished wood and carpets in traditional patterns. There were blue Delft plates arranged on one wall in the hall and the vases of flowers were unimaginative but charming.

Gil appeared suddenly, took a look around and made a discreetly amazed face at Chloe. This did not look like a house which often echoed to the sound of jazz.

'Oh, we mustn't forget Chloe,' Mr Haskell said, looking back and going a little pink at his own lapse in manners. 'I do beg your pardon, Chloe . . .'

She began to smile but the movement froze on her mouth as she saw Ben in the open doorway of the room beyond Mr Haskell. Ben was staring at her in scowling incredulity, his dark brows drawn together above his angry, dark blue eyes.

'What the hell . . .' he began in a harsh voice and his father stiffened.

'Ben!'

Ben switched his angry stare to Mr Haskell.

'I invited Chloe to sing tonight,' his father told him, and Ben's face tightened in speechless rage.

CHAPTER FOUR

'THE acoustics should be okay, anyway,' Gil murmured half an hour later as he quietly picked out a waltz on the grand piano in the drawing-room. His eye roamed over the eggshell blue walls and the high stuccoed ceiling on which white plaster cherubs flew at each corner, their round faces smugly beaming.

'The room's big enough,' Chloe agreed, leaning on the piano and wishing that she didn't feel a cold prickle down her spine warning her that Ben was watching them. He hadn't said a word after his father told him that Chloe was here on his invitation; he had seethed in silence for a minute then turned on his heel and walked back into the party with all the *joie de vivre* of someone going to a public hanging. Hetty had given Mr Haskell an admiring smile and he had looked ultra casual; asserting himself with his son while Hetty watched had obviously done wonders for his ego. Having been snubbed by Ben in his letter, Hetty was delighted to see Ben snubbed in his turn, of course, but Chloe had been less cheerful. Ben's glacial eyes had left her miserable. She had known it was a mistake to come, why had she let his father talk her into it?

'Big enough?' echoed Gil drily. 'My whole

85

flat's smaller than this room. What style would you call the decor? Mock Regency?'

'I suppose so. I'd guess the house was built around the turn of the century and the architect wanted a classical look; it's very Victorian in a way—just look at that white marble fireplace—it reminds me of a tomb, especially with that cherub poised overhead.'

'The guests have a graveyard look to them, too,' said Gil, and she laughed, shaking her head at him.

'Is that kind?' She had to admit that they looked rather dull, they were mostly of Mr Haskell's generation and made polite small talk as they sipped sherry and nibbled tiny pieces of smoked salmon in aspic or fragments of caviar and chopped egg on thin toast.

'A stuffy lot,' Gil said. 'Your mother's the only one who seems to be having a good time.'

They both looked at Hetty who was admiring a painting at the far end of the room; she had several male admirers in tow including Mr Haskell. Hetty was talking, they were laughing.

'She likes parties,' Chloe said with amused pride; her mother might be infuriating but she was never boring.

'She's fun,' Gil said, his long fingers permanently rippling over the keys. He was talking as if unaware of what his hands were doing, as if the music flowed through him without Gil needing to do a thing about it. 'I wish I could find a girl just like her.'

'Gil!' Chloe said with laughter. 'Shall I tell her

you're interested? Although I don't know how I feel about having you as a stepfather.'

'Hey!' Gil protested, going pink, then saw her teasing eyes and made a face. 'Oh, very witty. You know what I mean. And I'd have plenty of competition, wouldn't I? Starting with old Mr Haskell—he seems really smitten, he hasn't let her out of his sight since we got here. That son of his doesn't seem too pleased about it. Look at the way he's scowling now.'

Chloe didn't need to look—she could feel it, right through her shoulder blades.

'The old guy must be very rich,' Gil said thoughtfully. 'All those hotels! I suppose you can't blame his family for getting worried when he shows signs of spring fever. Seventy years old and he's acting like a kid. I hope I'm that lively when I'm seventy.'

'You're not that lively now!' Chloe told him.

'Watch it!' Gil said, grinning. He leaned towards her and kissed her cheek.

'What's that for?' Chloe asked, taken aback.

'I just love your whole family,' Gil said. 'I wish I could be adopted into it. My family never had such fun; yours is wonderful.'

'Your brain's going,' Chloe said, retreating with a smile. 'I'd better go and find out when Mr Haskell wants us to perform, while you're still able to play.'

'Kid, I can play when I'm unconscious,' Gil declared smugly.

'I know, I've seen you—but can you play when you're awake?' Chloe didn't wait for him to answer that, she walked away across the room, aware that the guests watched her while they talked to each other. They seemed slightly puzzled by her presence at the party. Everyone else was either a member of the family or connected with the business; none of them knew Chloe. Having seen Ben's family *en masse*, Chloe knew why he had never bothered to take her to meet them. They were stuffy, boring and faintly snobbish. Their voices had a monotone, well-bred note; their eyes were round and dull—if you looked them all over quickly they looked like rows of fish on a marble slab, glazed of eye and gaping-mouthed.

The one exception, of course, was Ben—he was wandering around in a restless fashion, picking up small ornaments, staring at them blankly and putting them down again while, every so often, he looked at Chloe and Gil. As she walked away from the piano, Chloe deliberately took a route which would take her past Ben. He watched her coming, his eyes moving over the sway of her body in the green silk dress which lovingly followed every curve of her figure.

'Having fun?' she asked as she drew level with him, knowing that she was waving a red flag at a bull.

Ben charged, as expected, catching hold of her arm. 'What are you doing here tonight? How did you meet my father?'

'Ask him,' Chloe said. She looked down at the hand which held her upper arm, his powerful fingers were pressed deep into her flesh. 'Let go of me.'

'Or what?' he sneered, tightening his grip.

She wanted to slap his hostile face, but she didn't lose her temper. She bent her knee and lifted one foot, softly rubbing her leg against his calf. Ben's eyes narrowed in surprise, he went red.

'My shoes have stiletto heels,' Chloe said in a honeyed voice. 'And if you don't take your hand off my arm I'll show you why the heels are called stilettos. You wouldn't be able to walk for a week.'

'You vixen,' Ben said, but he laughed shortly and released her.

Chloe lowered her foot again and moved an inch away from him.

'My father never told me he'd met you,' Ben said impatiently. 'Why has he asked you and your mother here tonight? What's behind all this?'

'Stop playing prosecuting counsel. I told you— ask your father those questions.'

Ben seethed, staring at her. 'Okay, then who's the guy at the piano?' he asked.

'Strangely enough, he's my pianist,' Chloe retorted.

'Just that?' Ben's lip curled in a sneer and she was furious with him.

She could have told him that Gil was, indeed, just that; but pride kept her silent. Ben looked at her with the eyes of an enemy, he wanted to hurt her. Why should she admit that there hadn't really been a man in her life since she and Ben split up? She had dated someone occasionally but it hadn't meant a thing—that discovery would probably give Ben a big kick, but she wasn't about to sacrifice her ego to his. There had to be a limit to how much emotional damage she could let him do to her in revenge for the hurt she had inflicted on him three years ago.

She shrugged without answering and Ben's eyes probed her face remorselessly, looking for the reply she hadn't given. Chloe was equally intent on his expression, her heart beating with sickening speed. Was he jealous? Did he still care about her? The thought made her dizzy, but the silence between them was too tense. She had to say something to break it up.

'You didn't tell me that your father was a jazz fan?'

'Didn't I? Maybe I didn't remember, or the subject never came up,' Ben said, then his mouth twisted and that cold look iced his eyes. 'I had other things on my mind at the time.' He watched her and she knew he was trying to needle her—his anger hadn't diminished, it had simply changed character, become a deliberate icy mockery which sought to hurt.

She tried to hide her own reaction to that; in *wanting* to hurt her, Ben did hurt. If he felt anything for her he wouldn't look at her with those distant, inimical eyes.

'Your sisters don't look much like you, do they?' she asked unsteadily. She had met them when she first arrived. They had seemed pleasant enough, but neither of them had said much.

Chloe hadn't been certain whether they were distant because they knew of her past relationship with Ben, or because they merely were not interested in her.

'Joan's like me in character, I'm told,' Ben said brusquely. His elder sister was nearly forty, a tall woman with a strongly featured face and short brown hair showing signs of grey.

'And Sybil's the one who is wearing the gorgeous Antony Price dress,' Chloe said and Ben glanced over his shoulder to where his younger sister was sitting with her husband and several of the other guests.

'Is that what it is? I wouldn't know,' he said, with a flash of real amusement. 'I'm not a fashion freak.'

'It's lovely,' Chloe said with faint envy, knowing she wouldn't have been able to afford the strikingly original black and gold dress; it demanded flare just to wear it, the fine pleats and daring neckline insisted on a good figure and tremendous assurance. Sybil had both, she also had her brother's colouring and an arrogant air of being ultra confident.

Ben's eyes moved over the dress she herself was wearing and she felt a hot pulse beating in her throat as he stared at the deep neckline, the shadowy cleft between her half-revealed breasts. There was sensual awareness in Ben's dark blue eyes, his hard mouth parted as though he was having difficulty breathing. She heard the deep inward breath he took and was suddenly agitated.

'I must go and ask your father when he wants

me to sing,' she said hurriedly, moving away. But she was running, and she knew it, because she couldn't face him without betraying her own fierce excitement, and at the moment they had a large audience, the room was crowded with people who had been watching them curiously as they talked. Chloe didn't know how much Ben's family knew of what had happened between them but she was in no hurry to find out.

'Oh, hello, dear,' Hetty said reluctantly, when Chloe joined her and Mr Haskell. If she had had a fan, she would have been fluttering it, thought Chloe with amused affection. She was having a wonderful evening, that was obvious.

'Ready to sing?' Mr Haskell asked. 'Shall I introduce you?'

'That would be nice,' Chloe said and made her way back to the piano, ignoring Ben's intent eyes as she passed him.

Mr Haskell clapped his hands and silence fell, the guests all turned to stare at him with polite smiles.

'I've always loved jazz,' he said, glancing around the circle of faces. 'So on my seventieth birthday I've decided to give myself a special present by having Chloe Tyrrell to sing at my party. I'm sure you're all going to enjoy her music as much as I do.'

'So there,' Gil murmured drily under his breath.

Chloe smiled sideways at him; there had been an element of warning in Mr Haskell's voice and the stiff reluctance on the faces of the guests as they began to find seats and settle down to listen made it clear that she wasn't going to have a wildly enthusiastic audience. Mr Haskell turned towards the piano and began to clap as he and Hetty moved forward to sit down among the rest of the party.

Gil began to play a Billie Holiday standard of which Chloe was very fond; it was fast and funny and demanded perfect timing but she had often sung it before and she knew every twist and turn of the music.

The chandelier glittered overhead, making the jewellery worn by some of the guests flash. Chloe's eyes roamed over the faces turned towards her; most of them middle-aged or older. Ben was leaning against a chair, his arms folded and his dark face impassive, she did not let her gaze dwell on him. His sisters sat with their husbands; Joan was staring at Chloe but Sybil was carefully twisting the thin tasselled belt she wore around her waist. She looked bored. One of the men had already fallen asleep before Chloe got to the end of her song. There was a brief pause then Mr Haskell began to clap enthusiastically, the others joined in with polite applause and the sleeping man woke up and snorted, looking around him in drowsy surprise.

Chloe's second song had been chosen deliberately—'What a Difference a Day Makes' had a wry poignancy which throbbed in her husky voice and made Ben straighten and watch her, his features unreadable. She didn't look at him directly but several times she let her eyes drift past him; she wanted to know if the song spoke to him but she couldn't tell anything from that cool mask. The only clue she got was that he listened intently and he wasn't lounging against the chair in front of him, as he had during the first song.

Mr Haskell had asked her to sing three songs so she finished with another lively number. That got her a genuine ripple of applause and nobody slept through it.

Mr Haskell thanked her and came over to kiss her on the cheek, handing her a glass of champagne. His daughters joined them, smiling.

'You're very *good*,' Sybil said, sounding surprised.

Chloe laughed. 'Thank you.'

'I've never been a jazz fan, myself,' said Joan, looking at Gil as he ran his hands over the keys. 'But I must say I enjoyed those songs. I like operetta—you know—*The Merry Widow*? That sort of thing?'

Gil grinned and began to play some Lehar and Joan exclaimed. 'That's it, such good tunes—I like music that *is* musical.'

'Joan plays the piano,' Sybil said and her sister went pink and made disclaiming noises but Gil stopped playing and shifted along the piano stool, gesturing to her to sit down next to him. 'Oh, no, no,' Joan said, flustered.

'She's not bad, oh, go on, Joan, don't be so silly!' Sybil said, amused. 'You know you're dying to play.'

'I'm just an amateur,' Joan said.

'We'll play Chopsticks, then,' Gil offered,

seizing her hand and pulling her down on the stool.

Everyone crowded around the piano, laughing now because Joan was one of them and they were much more interested in her than they had been in Chloe's professional performance. Chloe drank her champagne, listening to Gil and Joan giving a lively version of Chopsticks, then they began to play a song from an operetta and Chloe saw Ben turn and walk out of the room.

She put down her glass and pushed past the smiling guests—where was Ben going? As she went out into the hall she saw him disappearing through the front door, and followed like Alice in pursuit of the White Rabbit, and with as little common sense. She didn't stop to ask herself what she thought she was doing, chasing a man who was always walking away from her. She knew she would have no peace until she found out for certain whether his father was right or not—she had to know if Ben still cared for her. Wasn't it crazy to let the past come between them?

The moon has risen in the dark night sky, there was a cool wind blowing through the leafless trees, and Chloe shivered as she hovered on the gravelled drive, looking around for Ben. Had he driven off? Was she too late?

Then she saw him, walking along a path on the other side of a lawn, his head bent and his hands thrust deep into his pockets. Chloe crossed the lawn, her footsteps muffled by the damp grass; she couldn't walk fast in her very high heels, the earth was slippery with dew. Suddenly Ben seemed to hear her, he swung, startled, and Chloe halted, her heart crashing into her ribs. Now that she faced him she hadn't a clue what to say.

His face went through a variety of expressions; she couldn't read most of them but she suspected rage was paramount—the one he settled for, however, was cynical mockery and that she interpreted without difficulty.

'Are you following me?' he asked.

'Why would I do that?' Chloe stood very still, willing him to walk back towards her. Her hands curled at her sides, she put all her will power into an intent concentration on him. When he slowly came closer she felt elated, and her eyes glittered in the moonlight.

Ben stared at her, his face tightening. 'God knows,' he said. 'You tell me.'

'It was so hot in the party. I came out for some air.'

'It's cold out here!' Ben said disbelievingly.

'I'm not,' she said and heard him take a sharp breath.

'Aren't you? Sure about that?' His voice was low and husky and suddenly they weren't talking about the temperature in the garden. He put a hand on her bare arm and Chloe raised languid, passionate eyes to him. He stared into them, his fingers stroking her skin.

'You're being rather reckless,' he said flatly but the hand touching her was unsteady, she felt his fingertips dew with perspiration and his facial bones were taut with a self-control she sensed he

YOUR
DREAMS
CAN
COME
TRUE

H·A·R·L·E·Q·U·I·N
FIRST·CLASS
Sweepstakes

Enter and you can win a

◆ ROLLS-ROYCE™   ◆ TRIP TO PARIS   ◆ MINK COAT

TO EXPERIENCE A WORLD OF ROMANCE.

How to Enter Sweepstakes & How to get 4 FREE BOOKS, A FREE TOTE BAG and A BONUS MYSTERY GIFT.

1. Check ONLY ONE OPTION BELOW.
2. Detach Official Entry Form and affix proper postage.
3. Mail Sweepstakes Entry Form before the deadline date in the rules.

H·A·R·L·E·Q·U·I·N
FIRST·CLASS
Sweepstakes

OFFICIAL ENTRY FORM

Check one:

☐ Yes. Enter me in the Harlequin First Class Sweepstakes and send me 4 FREE HARLEQUIN PRESENTS® novels plus a FREE Tote Bag and a BONUS Mystery Gift. Then send me 8 brand new HARLEQUIN PRESENTS® novels every month as they come off the presses. Bill me at the low price of $1.75 each (a savings of $0.20 off the retail price). There are no shipping, handling or other hidden charges. I understand that the 4 Free Books, Tote Bag and Mystery Gift are mine to keep with no obligation to buy.

☐ No. I don't want to receive the Four Free HARLEQUIN PRESENTS® novels, a Free Tote Bag and a Bonus Gift. However, I do wish to enter the sweepstakes. Please notify me if I win.

108–CIP–CAJ3

See back of book for official rules and regulations.
Detach, affix postage and mail Official Entry Form today!

FIRST NAME_____ LAST NAME_____
                                    (Please Print)

ADDRESS_____ APT._____

CITY_____

PROV./STATE_____ POSTAL CODE/ZIP_____
"Subscription Offer limited to one per household and not valid to current Harlequin Presents® subscribers. Prices subject to change."

ENTER THE H·A·R·L·E·Q·U·I·N
FIRST·CLASS *Sweepstakes*

Detach, Affix Postage and Mail Today!

Harlequin First Class Sweepstakes
P.O. Box 52010
Phoenix, AZ 85072-9987

had difficulty maintaining. 'You had better go back into the house,' he added. 'Why run a pointless risk?'

'Aren't *you* cold?' she asked him with a faint smile and lifted a hand to his cheek; it wasn't cool, it almost burnt her skin to touch it, and she felt Ben recoil fiercely. He pushed her hand away on a reflex action but if he wanted to convince her that he was indifferent to her he was too late; she had heard his breathing quicken, seen the leap of desire in his eyes. He snatched his hand from her arm and turned away in the same movement.

'Go back to the party,' he said harshly as he walked away. Chloe watched him vanish behind some trees before she slowly went back to the house, and she was smiling as she walked.

Nobody seemed to have noticed her absence, they were all too busy crowding around the piano, swaying to the waltz tune Gil and Joan were playing. Chloe sank down on a couch to watch and a few moments later her mother noticed her and came over to join her.

'My feet are killing me,' Hetty said, slipping off her shoes and wriggling her toes with a sigh of relief. She waved a hand towards the piano. 'Now that's what I call music—why can't you sing that sort of stuff? That's easy on the ear.'

'Easy on the brain, too,' Chloe said wryly.

Mr Haskell missed Hetty and looked around for her, he came trotting towards them like a lost lamb looking for the flock. 'Are you tired?' he asked dividing the question between them.

'A little,' Chloe said with a smile.

'Certainly not,' said Hetty, deftly resuming her shoes before he noticed her stockinged feet.

Mr Haskell sat down on the other side of Hetty. 'This has been the best party I've had for years,' he said. 'Thanks to you two—I can't tell you how much I appreciate having had the pleasure of your company tonight.' The formality of his phrasing didn't lessen the real warmth of his voice and that quick smile. 'I hope you've both enjoyed it as much as I have.'

'It's been wonderful,' Hetty said.

Chloe smiled and nodded. Looking at her watch, she said: 'But I'm afraid we ought to be going soon—I have to work tomorrow night and Gil and I rehearse in the mornings.'

'Have you got a long contract with that club?' asked Mr Haskell.

'No, it ends quite soon—then I'm going to have a holiday. I haven't had a real break for years.'

Mr Haskell ran a slightly shaky hand over his thin hair. Chloe saw the blue veins standing out at his wrist, the swollen knuckles, and felt a dart of anxiety. He was so frail—was all this excitement good for him?

'I saw you talking to Ben,' he said. 'Wasn't I right?' He smiled, watching her eagerly, and she sighed.

'About what?' demanded Hetty, staring from one to the other.

'I'm not sure,' Chloe admitted. Ben had given her contradictory signals—yet were they really so very irreconcilable? He was bitter, he was angry with her—but she remembered that look in his eyes and she was certain that she still had the power to make his heart beat faster.

'What? What are you talking about?' Hetty insisted.

'Later, my dear, I'll tell you all about it later,' Mr Haskell soothed, patting her hand. He looked across her at Chloe. 'Did you know we've now got a hotel in Venice?'

Puzzled, she said: 'Yes, I saw something about it on television.' If Jilly hadn't seen Ben that morning she might never have confessed the truth, and that was frightening. How could Chloe have known that by switching on the TV set she was changing the whole course of her life? How terrifying that such a tiny action could be so important!

'The hotel opens in two weeks time. Chloe, how would like to star in the cabaret there?'

Chloe was so taken aback that she stammered: 'Well . . . that's very flattering, but . . .'

'I won't be there for the opening, I'm afraid,' Mr Haskell interrupted. 'But Ben will.' He paused and Chloe's mouth rounded into a surprised circle. He smiled at her. 'It's part of our board's policy that each new hotel is personally supervised by Ben for the first month, to make sure that it is running smoothly and everything is up to standard.'

Hetty was staring at them both and frowning; but Chloe didn't look at her mother. Her mind worked rapidly as she stared intently at Mr Haskell.

'You haven't discussed this idea with Ben, of course?'

'I'm still supposed to be the boss,' he said complacently. 'I don't have to ask Ben's permission before I hire a singer for a new hotel.'

'He'll be furious when he finds out!'

'Are you afraid of him, Chloe?' asked Mr Haskell and she laughed.

'He can be daunting, but . . .'

'But you still want to find out whether my hunch is right?' asked his father with a satisfied smile. 'Good, then it's a deal?'

'Is this some sort of conspiracy?' Hetty demanded.

'A very well-intentioned one,' Mr Haskell said.

'They're the most dangerous kind,' said Chloe with a worried sigh. 'And I ought to warn you— Ben's going to want an explanation of how you met me and why you invited me to sing here tonight. He has already asked me.'

'And what did you tell him?'

'Nothing,' Chloe said, laughing.

'I can see you know how to treat a man,' Ben's father said, winking.

'I'm my mother's daughter,' Chloe murmured and Hetty gave her an indignant glare.

'Don't you tar me with the same brush as yourself! Your father was a very happy man, let me tell you.'

'I'm sure he was,' said Mr Haskell in an admiring voice which made Chloe look at him with a mixture of amusement and compunction; somebody ought to warn him that Hetty was not always as sweet as honey, but then he was a grown man, he could take care of himself.

CHAPTER FIVE

TEN days later, Chloe's Alitalia jet touched down at Venice airport and she made her way through customs, wheeling her trolley, out into the cool misty morning which veiled the lagoon and hid Venice from her as she stood on the jetty outside the airport, staring across the water. The other passengers had left to take a coach but Mr Haskell had promised that the Hotel Luxor's own water taxi would pick her up and take her to the city across the lagoon instead of by road.

She was alone on the jetty and there was no sign of the promised boat, but while she hesitated, wondering if she should make other arrangements to get to the hotel, she heard the throb of an engine and then a sleek black and gold boat cut through the mist, heading towards her. Chloe leaned on her trolley, watching the tall boatman who was steering, one hand on the tiller, his long body swaying to the motion of the boat. Was that the hotel uniform? she wondered, noticing the navy-blue fisherman's jersey and white pants he wore. She couldn't see his face, only the ruffled black hair which blew in the wind, but suddenly she stiffened in shock. It couldn't be Ben. It was very like him, but it couldn't be.

Mr Haskell had told her that Ben wouldn't be

at the hotel when she arrived, he had been recalled to London yesterday on urgent business. That had been a pretext by Mr Haskell to get Ben away from Venice for long enough to give Chloe a chance of settling in at the hotel. His father promised her that Ben wouldn't order her to leave when he came back and discovered that she was there.

'He may not be too pleased when he finds out that I've asked you to sing at the hotel for a month, but he won't go against my wishes,' Mr Haskell had said confidently.

Chloe hoped his confidence was justified, she had her doubts. Narrowing her eyes she tried to make out the features of the man speeding towards her. Her imagination could be playing tricks—every dark-haired man she saw wasn't going to be Ben. Of course, she was nervous, she wasn't sure she was wise in coming here; but whenever she began to thing about backing out she remembered Ben's eyes when she touched his cheek in the garden on the night of his father's birthday party. Ben was stubborn and unyielding, he was still bitterly angry with her, but if there was any chance—however remote and unlikely—that Ben would one day forgive her and be prepared to try again, she had to take it. She had no doubts at all about how she felt; she loved him, if she lost him she would never care this much about another man. This might be a battle she could not win, but she was fighting for her life and the risk of getting hurt wasn't going to stop her.

The black and gold boat slowed and glided alongside, the boatman turned and looked up and Chloe's heart turned over with a sickening speed as she saw his face. Her cheeks began to burn.

Ben leapt out and tied up deftly, ignoring her for a moment. When he turned Chloe's heart sank at the hostile look in his blue eyes.

'Hallo,' she said huskily, trying a smile which visibly wavered. She glanced down at the trolley. 'This is my luggage, I'll take one case if you can manage the others.'

'You're getting back on a plane to London,' Ben informed her curtly.

Her hands closed over the handle of one case. She lifted her chin defiantly. 'I have a legal contract to sing at your hotel and I've come a long way today, I intend to fulfil my contract.'

'You'll be paid,' Ben said harshly. 'But you won't be singing at my hotel.'

'Your father . . .'

'My father had no right to offer you a job!' Ben's brown skin was drawn tightly over his cheekbones, his eyes were chips of blue ice. He confronted her, his lean body poised as though he was on the edge of violence, and she was slightly scared of him. In the navy-blue jersey and casual pants he looked tough and dangerous—not a man to argue with or ignore. She couldn't hold his eyes, she had to look away.

'Didn't he tell you that he had offered me this job?' she murmured, pretending bewilderment. She certainly couldn't risk admitting that she had known that his father had conspired with her to keep it a secret.

'No, he didn't,' Ben said curtly. 'I can't imagine why he offered it to you. We don't need a singer. The only music we'll be having is a small band, they'll play in the evenings for guests who want to dance after dinner. There were no plans for a cabaret.'

'I see,' Chloe said, eyes still lowered. Hadn't he gone to London, after all? Why hadn't his father warned her that Ben would be at the hotel when she got there?

'I saw my father in London yesterday, but he didn't mention your name. I flew back early this morning and the boatman mentioned that a singer was coming in on this flight. I checked up with the manager, then I rang London.' His mouth twisted angrily. 'My father was not available—in a meeting, they said.' He laughed as if he would like to hit somebody. 'He must have realised that I'd found out what he'd been up to.'

Chloe glanced at him through her lashes and to her alarm saw his face change, a watchful tension come into his eyes.

'He must be out of his mind,' Ben said softly and if she hadn't liked his expression five minutes ago, she liked it even less now. His mouth was curving in sharp cynicism and those cold blue eyes had a sardonic glitter to them.

'Now, I wonder why he's so keen to promote your career?' he asked as if talking to himself, arching his brows.

Chloe didn't answer—he had obviously realised

that his father was trying to heal the breach between them, and the idea was giving him angry amusement, judging by his expression.

'Well, well,' he drawled. 'I'd never have expected it of my father. He's never been a fool where women were concerned, but then he is getting old. I suppose I should have realised there could be problems now that he's more or less retired and at a loose end—but I certainly hadn't expected him to lose his head over a girl young enough to be his granddaughter.'

Chloe gasped in disbelief at the end of that sentence, heat beginning to burn in her face.

'Don't be ridiculous!' she burst out, looking up.

'You took the word right out of my mouth,' Ben murmured with a trace of malice. 'Ridiculous just about describes it.' He leaned towards her menacingly. 'If you have any crazy idea of becoming my stepmother, you can forget it. I'd fight tooth and nail to stop it happening.'

Shaking with rage, Chloe faced him, head up. 'Your mind is disgusting!'

'Thank you—coming from you, that's quite a compliment,' he threw back.

'Your father is a wonderful old man . . .'

'*Old* man,' Ben repeated. 'Very old, remember.'

'Oh, shut up,' Chloe seethed. 'The very idea of him . . . I ought to slap your face.'

'Try it,' Ben encouraged, bending closer, and Chloe might have done it if she hadn't seen the warning glitter of his eyes. Discretion seemed the better part of valour. She got the distinct impression that Ben was yearning to do something violent to her and she wasn't going to give him the chance. She turned away, consumed with anger, and picked up a case, flinging it down into the boat, which rocked wildly at the impact. Chloe grabbed another one and Ben shot forwards, snarling.

'What the hell do you think you're doing?'

She held on to the handle of the case, tugging. Ben gripped it too, pulling it towards him.

'I'm not standing here arguing with you all day. I'm tired and I want to get to the hotel.' She gave a fresh yank on the handle and Ben stumbled into her as the case dragged him with it. Chloe was startled into dropping the handle. The case landed with a thud on Ben's toe, and he fell back with a grunt of pain. While he was otherwise occupied, giving vent to a few stifled swear words, Chloe lifted the case and dropped that, too, down into the boat. Waves washed up the wooden steps. Chloe ignored them, running quickly down to step into the boat. She was huddled inside the cabin before Ben had joined her.

He leaned in to stare at her, supporting himself with one hand on the cabin roof. 'Very well, you might as well stay the night, since you refuse to go back today, but first thing tomorrow I'll get you on a plane back to London.'

Chloe kept her profile towards him, staring fixedly through the window opposite at the misty distances of the lagoon. After a moment Ben growled under his breath and stamped off to start the engine.

They sped across the water, spray leaping around the boat and a chill wind blowing Chloe's hair in all directions. She strongly suspected Ben of going too fast, on purpose; but if he could stand an uncomfortable boat ride so could she. She refused to complain, she pretended not to have noticed that she was bumping around on the leather-padded seat or that her face was wet with spray and her hair dewed with it.

Ben's speed slowed after ten minutes; either because he was ashamed of having lost his temper or because they were rapidly approaching the city. Craning her neck Chloe could see the pale domes of the church of Santa Maria della Salute. They rose out of the mist as if they floated in mid-air without a building to support them, but then the sun broke through and the boat bucketed across the green-blue water while all of Venice began to shape itself in front of her dazzled eyes. She excitedly picked out familiar silhouettes—the green spire of the Campanile rising into the sky, the lacy white and pink stonework of the Doge's Palace with its arches and pillared balcony, the domes of the Basilica rising behind it, and crowding behind St Mark's the terracotta roofs and coloured walls of the hundreds of other buildings in the city.

Ben glanced back over his shoulder, his face relaxed now. 'The sun has come out.'

She got up and joined him, watching how, with the sunlight gleaming on it, the water took on a

new colour—a vivid aquamarine, above which the
flying spray glittered and danced. Ahead of them
she saw the lion-topped column at the start of the
Piazzetta which led to St Mark's; a bell rang
somewhere and pigeons flew upwards from the
square into the bright blue sky. Half turning to
look back Chloe could see where the mist still
cloaked the distance; the city lay in sunlight,
though, and she felt her spirits lift as her
shoulder brushed Ben's and he glanced down
sideways at her, black lashes barring his brown
cheek.

'Isn't it beautiful?' Chloe murmured, her eyes
riveted not by the city but by Ben's hard-boned
profile. Venice did not make her heart beat faster,
but Ben did, even when he was frowning with
hostility. Now, though, he seemed calm, his
mouth had a warm curve to it and she felt a fierce
dart of passion at the memory of that mouth
touching her own. Love ached inside her and she
looked away, trembling.

Ben brought the boat alongside the hotel jetty
and a young man in a smart livery ran to help
him tie-up at one of the freshly painted black and
gold striped poles. Ben leapt out and turned to
hand Chloe up on the jetty. She felt his fingers
close firmly round her own but they dropped
away the minute she was safely on dry land.
Leaving the porter to bring her luggage into the
hotel, Ben strode away and she followed him
through high glass doors, along a marble-floored
hall full of comfortable armchairs to the reception
desk.

The hotel was quietly opulent; with glassy marble floors on which had been laid wide bands of dark red carpet, pale pink marble walls on which hung gilt-framed mirrors and dark oil paintings, pink brocade covered chairs arranged in fours with low marble-topped tables between them and overhead the famous Murano chandeliers with their clusters of pink roses from which spilled chiming, glittering waterfalls of silvery glass. Listening, Chloe could hear nothing but the measured ticking of a grandfather clock. You could tell that the hotel was empty. The staff moved quietly and a raised voice made you jump.

'Miss Tyrrell's room is ready for her?' Ben asked the clerk behind the wide mahogany topped desk.

'Certainly, sir,' the young man said eagerly, producing a key.

'You'd better give him your passport and sign the Foreign Visitor's form for the police,' Ben decided curtly.

'If Miss Tyrrell is working here . . .' the clerk began.

'Just take her passport and check her into the hotel as a guest, for the moment,' Ben interrupted. He picked up the key. 'I'll take her up—send up the luggage when they get it all in.'

Chloe was angry—Ben's terse tone had made the reception clerk look at her curiously. Flushed, she turned away to walk towards the steel lift. It opened as she came towards it and a group of young men emerged, talking cheerfully to each other in Italian. They were all in their early twenties, had black hair and eyes, and wore casual coloured tops and cotton pants in the latest fashion. Chloe stepped aside to let them pass, but to her surprise they halted to stare at her.

'Hi! You Chloe?' one said, his accent only faintly marked.

Taken aback, she nodded, then hurriedly smiled. 'Yes—how did you know?'

'We're the band.' Smiling, the young man held out his hand. 'I'm Angelo—I play keyboard and I run this outfit.'

The others made cheerful noises of disagreement, but they grinned at her as Angelo introduced them.

'This is Georgio, he plays drums; Nino's our guitarist and Paolo . . . well, he plays everything.'

Chloe shook hands, taking in a brief impression of each—Georgio was short and very skinny, with a mop of thick black hair and a very large nose; Nino was very tall and almost as thin as Georgio but his body had a loose-limbed grace that Georgio lacked, and Paolo was the youngest of them, his face was vivacious, eager, outgoing.

'How did you know about me?' Chloe asked.

'The desk clerk,' Angelo shrugged.

'Your English is very good,' she told him and he looked pleased.

'Sure, I live in England two years, working as a barman—trying to get jobs as a musician but no good so I come back, start my own band and we do okay here.'

'Have you got a singer?' she asked and they looked warily at her.

'Nino, he sings a little, but he plays guitar better,' Angelo said, ducking as Nino aimed a punch at him. 'Okay, okay, Nino, but it's a sin to tell a lie,' he teased.

Looking back at Chloe, he said carefully: 'You want to sing with us?'

Chloe wasn't sure how to answer that. She smiled at him. 'I sing jazz.'

Their faces cleared. 'Jazz? Right—we play rock, you know?'

Chloe was amused by their obvious relief. 'I'll enjoy listening to you,' she told them. 'But I only sing jazz—each to his own.'

Angelo's English didn't run to that. He stared, baffled, working it out. 'Oh, right,' he said and, watching him, Chloe thought that he must be the most beautiful man she had ever seen—yet oddly he had no sexual attraction for her whatever. His features had a classical perfection of proportion which was softened by his smooth, olive skin and sweet-natured smile into an almost feminine beauty. It was, strangely enough, his very sweetness of character that barred his looks from making an impact with women—his mouth was too gentle, his lustrous black eyes too soft, for his face to be forcefully male.

'But I was told that there would be a pianist here who would play for me,' Chloe added questioningly.

They look blank, then Angelo said: 'I guess I could work with you—I can play piano and I did some jazz, but I'm not too hot at that stuff.'

Chloe bit her lip. Mr Haskell had promised her

that there would be a jazz pianist at the hotel. Had he meant Angelo?

The band's faces changed suddenly, they muttered vaguely about having to go and moved off in a rush. Chloe looked round to find Ben at her elbow, his expression forbidding. He walked past her into the lift and she followed after a second. Had he given Angelo and his friends a filthy look? she wondered. He hadn't smiled, she could be sure of that. He jabbed the button and the lift doors closed. As they smoothly rose, Chloe stared at his rigid profile, resenting his stony silence and the way he was jangling her key ring, which hung from one of his fingers. He was in a temper again.

They got out at the second floor and walked along a wide corridor. Ben unlocked a door and stood back to let her enter. 'They've put you in one of the best rooms on this floor,' he said, then added brusquely: 'My father's orders—not mine!' as if afraid of what she might read into being given such a good room.

'You didn't need to underline that,' Chloe said with a dry smile, looking around her. The shutters were closed, Ben silently strode over and flung them back, letting sunlight flood in, showing her the wide bed with its heavy pink brocade coverlet, the pale green silk wallpapered walls, the lacquered furniture which was the black and gold of the hotel's colours and the familiar Murano chandelier which hung everywhere in Venice.

'Your balcony looks out over the Grand

Canal,' Ben said, with his back to her, staring out.

She walked over to join him and felt him stiffen. Sliding a sideways glance at him she saw the rigidity of his cheekbones, the hooded fixity of his eyes as he stared straight ahead, trying to pretend he wasn't aware of her. Deliberately Chloe let her shoulder brush his, she leaned forward to stare out and her cheek was inches away from his face. She saw the pale domes of Santa Maria della Salute again.

'Isn't that the Salute?'

'Yes, you know it is,' Ben said tersely, turning to look at her with cool sarcasm.

They looked into each other's eyes. She saw his waver, she heard the quickening of his breathing, and the blood ran faster in her veins. Very slowly she put a hand up to his face to push back a ruffled strand of black hair which had been blown across his cheek. Ben was staring down at her mouth. His nostrils were flared, his face slightly darkened with blood. His head moved at a snail's pace, lowering towards her, and Chloe tilted her head, her hand gently moving along his throat, around to the back of his nape to press his head down to meet her lips.

For one second she felt Ben resisting, the muscles beneath her fingers were tensed, then her mouth softly brushed over his and he gave a muffled groan. His hand came up and clasped the back of her head, his other hand caught at her waist, and then his mouth covered her lips with a force that made her gasp. She felt his long fingers tangling in her hair, their grip almost painful, and his kiss became an assault, a punishment, he wasn't making love to her, he was making war.

Angrily, Chloe tried to push him away, wriggling and pummelling his broad shoulders, but he was too strong, she couldn't shift him. She felt him begin unbuttoning her black silk shirt, and when she tried to thrust his fingers away he trapped her between his muscular thighs and bent her backwards, keeping her off balance, her head thrown back under the onslaught of that fierce kiss and her body helpless.

When his hand slid inside her opened shirt and touched her bare breast she felt heat run through her veins and her furious struggles weakened.

Ben's mouth moved from her lips and pressed into her pulsing throat. 'I still want you—isn't that what you've been trying to find out?' he muttered, his teeth grazing her skin. 'Well, now you know. Your body can still turn me on and as it's on offer I see no reason why I shouldn't take it, but that is as far as it goes.' He lifted his head, still holding her backwards, and her eyes met the blue steel of his stare, her body shuddering with pain at the way he was looking at her. His eyes pierced and rejected her and Chloe felt tears burning behind her lids. 'I don't make the same mistake twice,' Ben said bitterly. 'I'll go to bed with you but I'll never feel the same way as I did. If sex is all you want . . .'

'No!' Chloe broke out harshly, shivering with icy cold.

'Sure?' Ben's hard mouth had a cynical twist

that made her feel even worse, but before he could say anything else there was a tap on the door, and Ben shot a look towards it, frowning, then lifted her to her feet and began to walk away, brushing a hand over his ruffled hair.

'You'd better go into the bathroom,' he said over his shoulder. 'And tidy yourself up.'

Chloe almost ran across the room and bolted herself into the bathroom. She leaned on the door, tears running down her face, trembling with humiliation, pain and anger. Ben hated her—he wanted her, but there had been a cold dislike in his eyes as he told her that he would go to bed with her but he would never care for her again. She shouldn't have let his father talk her into pursuing him to Venice; it had been such an obvious conspiracy, she had laid herself open to the way Ben had just behaved. Did he really imagine that she would be prepared to go to bed with him, knowing how he felt? Was that the sort of woman he thought she was?

She heard Ben's deep tones in the room and then the sound of the door closing. The porter must have brought up her luggage. Chloe pulled herself together, rubbing a shaky hand over her wet face. She looked at herself in the floor length mirror beside the deep white bath, and winced at her own reflection. What did she look like? Her hair was tangled, her shirt hung open, her lipstick was smeared and her face hectically flushed and grubby with tearstains. She was grateful that the porter hadn't see her—God knows what he would have thought if he had walked in here and caught her in Ben's arms. Another second and the man might have used his key and entered without waiting to be told he could come in, and it made her sick to imagine how Ben might have smiled at her discomfort. He wanted to hurt her, of course; he wanted his revenge, and she was being fool enough to give him the chance of achieving his aim.

She did up her shirt with trembling hands, ran some cold water and splashed her hot face with it, dried her skin with roughness and flicked back her hair before she unbolted the door and nerved herself to face Ben. Somehow she had to look calm, to put on an act which might convince him, make him think that he hadn't shattered her self-confidence and wrecked all her hopes of persuading him to forgive her. There was a limit to how much punishment she could take for what she had done three years ago—and she had reached it.

She walked slowly into her bedroom and halted, looking around. Ben had left, she was alone, and in the silence she heard herself sigh—a deep, wrenched sigh more like a groan. She didn't cry again, she wasn't going to let Ben hurt her any more. Tomorrow she was getting back on the plane to London and she was going to forget she had ever known him.

CHAPTER SIX

HER luggage was neatly stacked on a wooden rack behind the door. Taking a deep breath, she marched over and picked up the top case. She wasn't going to let Ben get to her like this—she wouldn't even think about him, she would unpack and hang up her clothes. Okay, she thought defiantly, whisking silky, lacy lingerie out of a case and folding it neatly into a drawer, tomorrow she was going to have to pack these cases again and leave! In the meantime, she wasn't going to leave her stage costumes in their carriers or her jeans folded one on top of another, they would be creased beyond hope when she finally did unpack them.

When she had emptied the last case and the room was spotless again, she looked at her watch, her face distracted. 'Now what?' she asked herself. She wasn't hungry, she had eaten a snack on the plane. Standing in front of the mirror she said to her reflection: 'I'm going out—I'm in Venice, I might as well see it!' Her reflection looked knowing; Chloe made a furious face at it, then noticed that her clothes were travel-creased. She wasn't going out like that, she thought, whirling away to find something else to wear.

She changed into a candy pink cotton tunic and matching pants—with her hair briskly brushed and her lips glossed a candy pink she decided she looked less like someone in a state of advanced gloom. That was what she wanted—to look bright and uncaring! If Ben saw her, he wouldn't be able to smile derisively now. She grabbed up her camera and handbag and went downstairs.

There was no one about in the reception area except the clerk behind his desk. Chloe gave him a polite smile, halting. 'Which way do I go to get to St Mark's?' she asked and he gave her directions eagerly, leaning over to watch her walk away. She was impatiently conscious of his appraisal of her glossy brown hair, high breasts and the sway of her tall, supple body in the casual outfit. Chloe had never been pretty, her face was too strongly featured, but she had a graceful, sensual way of walking which was entirely natural and of which she was not conscious until she caught a man watching her. When she was on stage she deliberately accentuated her swaying walk, of course; but for some odd reason she lost her self-consciousness once she was singing. She had a totally different persona on stage, donning a mask behind which she could hide her self-doubts, her sense of personal inadequacy, her uncertainty about her own attraction.

She left the hotel by a different door to the one leading out on to the jetty. The hotel was long and narrow. This door led into a tiny square entirely surrounded by high walls, the backs of other buildings on three sides and the hotel on the fourth. Chloe walked across it to a small alley in the furthest corner, and at the end of that found herself in a wider street with shops on each side.

She was using her camera a moment later as she crossed the bridge outside the extraordinary church of San Moise, Holy Moses, with its heavy, baroque façade. Chloe leaned right back, her body supported by the low bridge, to get shots of the five statues poised along the roof edge of the church.

Suddenly someone stopped behind her and she looked upwards, her face startled, to see Angelo's olive-skinned face inverted above her.

'Crazy church,' he said with a grin. 'It makes me laugh.'

'I love it,' Chloe said, straightening and watching him take a step downwards on the bridge to join her.

'Sure, me too,' he agreed amiably. 'But crazy, right? You know who built it? The Fini family. For God? No, in Venice when you built a church it was to tell the world how rich, how important you were—all the top families built churches. The Barbarini built one even crazier than this— with themselves on the façade, big, big statues of them, and stuff about how important they were. Like advertisements, you know?'

Chloe laughed. 'I know. In the States the politicians buy TV time to give themselves a pat on the back.'

'Right,' said Angelo, falling into step with her as she made her way through the narrow street leading to the Piazza San Marco.

'Nothing changes, does it?'

Angelo made a face. 'Sure it does—people used to build beautiful churches and palaces, now they put up concrete matchbox offices instead.'

Chloe halted as they emerged from the shadows of the arcades into the long, sunlit rectangle of the square. She stared in admiration at the glitter of St Mark's mosaics above the arched doorways, the red brick of the Campanile with its green spire, the grey flutter of pigeons and on each side the three-storied buildings above the porticoed arcades. Tourists washed to and fro across the square, some halting to sit down at one of the open-air cafés whose yellow chairs spilled out across the pavement.

'Beautiful,' she murmured, taking rapid pictures.

'I take some of you?' Angelo offered, holding out a hand for the camera, and Chloe gave it to him and stepped back in the sunlight, smiling at him.

He took several pictures and then Chloe took one of him for which he posed, light-heartedly, a hand on the back of one of the yellow chairs.

'This your first trip to Venice?' asked Angelo and she laughed, shaking her head.

'I've been here once before, but I didn't see much of it.'

'Okay, you got yourself a guide,' he said happily. 'Did you go to Florian's?'

'No, what's that?'

'The oldest café in the world, I guess—eighteenth century and they haven't changed a thing. We have a drink there now, you'll love it.'

He put a hand under her elbow and guided her
into the arcade on the right hand of St Mark's.
The name Florian was written on faded gold leaf
above the windows. A waiter directed them to a
free table in one of the tiny rooms which opened
on from another, and they sat down on dark red
plush seats with a small marble-topped table in
front of them. Chloe gazed around, entranced by
the apple-green enamel on the walls, which were
hung with dim, smoky mirrors reflecting the
room as if everyone in it were ghosts. Sprays of
painted plaster flowers, pink and white, stood out
in relief here and there, and the ceiling was
painted and richly ornamented too.

They drank white wine and Angelo ate some
tiny macaroons while Chloe stared out of the
window at the sunlit square with its constant
traffic of tourists and pigeons.

'You know, when the Austrians occupied
Venice they drank their coffee at the café
opposite. The Venetians drank theirs in Florian's
and ignored the Austrians on the other side, they
even forbad their children to cheer the music the
Austrians played.' Angelo's eyes sparkled with
amusement and Chloe laughed.

'That must have been fun—a silent protest,
very stylish.' She looked at her watch. 'We've
been here half an hour,' she said in surprise. 'I'll
pay the bill, Angelo.'

He protested politely, but she insisted. 'After
all, you're my guide for the afternoon and I'm
grateful for being shown Venice by a Venetian.'

'*Grazie*,' Angelo bowed. 'I teach you a little

Italian, too, maybe.' He strolled out of the café while Chloe paid the bill, then they walked across the square and went into the Basilica of St Mark's. When they emerged, an hour later, Chloe blinked at the sunlight—her eyes were dazed by the gold and glitter of the mosaics in the great church. She had spent ten minutes staring at the incredible golden altar screen which was enriched by enamels and jewels, and Angelo had almost had to drag her away from her fascinated study of the ceilings with their barbaric, Byzantine saints whose black eyes and fierce faces glowed darkly among the golden mosaic.

'Want to see some shops now?' Angelo asked hopefully. 'Venice has great shops.'

She smiled, nodding, and he took her through narrow streets to look at shop windows; at elegant, hand-made shoes, silk dresses and scarves, beautifully embossed leather belts and handbags. In many of the windows carnival masks were displayed among the other goods, and when she asked Angelo about them he looked surprised.

'But Carnival begins next week!'

'Carnival? Here?' Chloe had had no idea.

'Sure, here,' he said, amused by her disbelief. 'Venice was famous for her Carnival—it went on for months, really, I'm serious—for months! Then it stopped; no more Carnival for years. Don't ask me why, I don't know!' He grinned as her mouth parted and closed, the question unasked. 'But now it's started up again—the students began it one year, it wasn't planned, you know, it just . . .' he waved a hand, searching for the right word, and Chloe supplied it helpfully.

'Happened?'

He laughed. 'Right. It just happened—now they have it every spring and students come to it from all over Italy. Art students make these masks, *papier mâché*, most of them—it gives them a few lire. Some of the masks are very clever.'

'Yes, aren't they?' Chloe said, staring at the *papier mâché* masks, most of them painted white but with splashes of gold or vivid colour across the cheeks, around the eyes or on the mouth. 'They aren't expensive, either, are they? I think I'll buy one.'

'They have a bigger selection on stalls in a square quite near here. I'll take you there, if you like. You'll see that everyone wears a mask during Carnival week. You can hire costumes too—or make your own.'

They strolled on and came out in St Mark's square again. Chloe stopped short, surprised, and Angelo laughed at her expression.

'Here, every alley leads to San Marco—eventually!'

'We've been going in circles,' Chloe said, ruefully.

'Tired?'

'Dead,' she admitted. 'I haven't walked so much for years. And I'm dying for a cup of tea.'

'Tea!' Angelo muttered, amused. 'The English and their tea! I don't understand it. Coffee, okay—but tea? No, not for me. But we'll go back to the hotel and they will make for you the tea.

You can sit down and soon you'll feel better, okay?'

As she nodded, walking on, a little group of teenagers who were running across the square almost knocked her over. Angelo caught hold of her waist, steadying her.

'Thanks,' she said, smiling at him.

'Okay,' he said in his light, amiable voice and Chloe thought again how little sexual attraction he had. Angelo was charming and kind-hearted, helpful and good-natured, but he was no ball of fire where women were concerned. There was a lot of the little boy in him; he appealed to the maternal instinct rather than the mating instinct.

They crossed the square, talking, Angelo's arm around her shoulders in a gently protective gesture which she accepted in the spirit in which it was offered, almost leaning against his slim shoulder.

It wasn't until they reached the far corner of the square, from which led the street which would take them back to the hotel, that Chloe saw Ben standing in the shadows of the arcade, his face a dark mask from which glittering blue eyes watched her, his lean body taut in the white silk shirt and cream linen pants he wore. Angelo didn't notice him, he was talking enthusiastically about the delights of Carnival week. Chloe briefly met Ben's angry stare then quickly looked away, tense with surprise and resentment. He stared at her as if he hated her; it made her want to cry again, but she wouldn't—she would never cry over Ben again.

'What are you going to do about getting a pianist?' Angelo asked as they finally reached the hotel. 'If you can't find one, I don't mind having a shot, okay?'

Chloe looked at him gratefully, his kindness was heart-warming in her mood of depression over the way Ben had stared at them a few moments ago.

'That's very kind of you, Angelo. I don't know yet whether I'm staying . . .'

He looked bewildered. 'No? I thought you were here for four weeks?'

'Mr Haskell and his father don't see eye to eye on that,' she said drily.

'Eye to eye?' repeated Angelo, even more baffled.

She laughed. 'It doesn't matter. Thank you for the offer and if I'm staying I'd love to take you up on it.'

'Okay,' he said easily. 'You know the hotel opens next weekend—if you're staying we got to rehearse soon?'

'Yes, of course, I'll let you know tomorrow.' Chloe sank into a chair in the spacious bar, and Angelo called the bar waiter over, and ordered a pot of tea for Chloe and a glass of lager for himself.

When she had drunk her tea, Chloe said goodbye to Angelo, thanked him for his tour of the city, and went up to her room to take a long bath. She lay back in the scented bubbles and wiggled her toes thoughtfully, staring at them, while she tried to decide what to do. She could ring Mr Haskell and tell him that Ben was ordering her to leave—but where was the point of that? Ben would make her life an ordeal if she stayed; she wasn't a masochist, she didn't enjoy getting hurt. She might as well admit defeat and catch a plane tomorrow.

Sighing, she climbed out of the bath and towelled herself lightly before slipping on the white towelling robe which hung on the door. Barefoot she wandered into her bedroom and stopped dead, her stomach plunging in shock as she saw Ben sitting on her bed.

'What are you doing in here?' she demanded in a voice high with nerves.

He ran assessing, insolent eyes over her from head to foot, missing nothing, and she was suddenly intensely aware of being naked under the brief robe. Ben's dark pupils seemed to reflect what he was seeing, the long, damp, shapely legs and bare pink feet, the pale throat and the cleft between her breasts which her robe left exposed. She clutched at the lapels urgently, dragging them together, and hated the mocking smile which drifted over his face at the gesture.

'I came to tell you that I've changed my mind,' he drawled. 'If my father wants you to sing at the hotel, he might as well have his way. It isn't worth arguing about. I don't want to quarrel with him about anything so unimportant.'

Chloe stood stiffly, struggling not to show her anger over the way he had phrased that. Unimportant? That was what she was, was it? She felt like chucking something at him but she refused to give in to the temptation especially while his lazy eyes were exploring the warm, white flesh she was trying vainly to hide.

'Very well,' she said coolly, as though indifferent to his decision.

Ben showed no sign of being ready to leave, however; he lounged on the bed, his body lithe and relaxed in the close-fitting white shirt and pants, his black hair gleaming as sunlight touched it and gave the strands a blue tinge.

'Enjoy your walk?' he asked, watching her through hooded lids.

'Very much.' Chloe felt herself tense as she remembered the way he had stared at her in St Mark's square. If he was going to look at her like that every time he saw her, the next four weeks were going to be agonising.

'Angelo's a native,' Ben told her, and she nodded.

'I know. He offered to play for me, by the way. Is that okay or had your father arranged for a jazz pianist to accompany me?'

Ben observed her, eyes narrowed. 'If he had, I haven't heard about it. Do you need a pianist?'

'Of course I do,' she almost snapped. 'A band would be even better, but failing that I must have some sort of music to sing to and I'd like to take Angelo up on his offer.'

Ben stood up and she almost flinched away from the reminder of how powerful his body was; the broad shoulders rippled with muscle under that thin shirt and his long, slim legs could move twice as fast as her own. Ben was a daunting opponent, both mentally and physically. Chloe's heart leapt into her throat as she watched him move towards her. She backed, swallowing, her hazel eyes bright green with alarm.

He looked at her sardonically. 'No need to look so wary. I'm not going to make love to you.'

Face burning, she said furiously: 'You wouldn't get the chance again—last time was quite enough, thank you.'

'You didn't seem to think so,' he murmured derisively, and she screwed her hands up at her sides to stop herself from hitting him. His eyes lowered to the neckline of her robe, which had fallen open again once she let go of the lapels, and with a muffled gasp of temper Chloe grabbed at it, holding it tightly and defensively.

'Get out of my room,' she ordered. 'And don't come in here again without knocking and waiting for me to open the door.'

'I did knock, there wasn't any answer—you were in the bath and didn't hear me, so I used the floor pass-key.'

'Well, don't use it again,' Chloe snapped. 'In future, I'll bolt my door. I don't want to come out of the bathroom and find you sitting on my bed again.'

His eyes glittered with mockery. 'Next time I might be in it,' he menaced softly, and Chloe took a sharp breath before darting quickly past him and flinging open the door.

'Will you please leave?'

Ben took his time, sauntering towards her lazily, that cool smile curving his mouth and his blue eyes watching her as though he was enjoying

her helpless rage. Chloe shrank back against the
wall as he drew level with her; the way he looked
at her made her feel as though he was touching
her, there was intimate insolence in that
flickering glance. He was silently mocking her
and there was nothing she could do to get back at
him; she had placed herself in this position. By
following Ben to Venice she had given him the
chance to torment her; she shouldn't have let his
father talk her into coming here, she shouldn't
have given in to her own craving to see Ben
again. She had put the weapons into his hand; she
shouldn't be surprised to find Ben using them.

'Dinner is at eight, by the way,' he murmured,
then he walked away and Chloe slammed the
door behind him and bolted it with a violence
that he must have heard.

She leaned on the wall, shaking with rage—
how dared he look at her like that, talk to her in
that derisive voice? She ought to pack and catch
that plane tomorrow. If she had any sense that
was what she would do; what point was there in
staying? She had persuaded herself that she
might be able to reach Ben if she was here, under
the same roof, for a month—but the way he had
acted just now had made it plain that there was
no way she could ever get him to change his mind
about her.

Why had Ben decided to let her stay? she
wondered suddenly, frowning. He had said it was
because he was not prepared to quarrel with his
father over her, and that was probably true. They
were obviously very close; Ben wouldn't want to

have an open row with Mr Haskell. She had a flash of intuition—had Ben decided to get his own way in some other fashion? He wanted her to go, but he didn't want to order her to leave in case he offended his father—if it was Chloe who broke the contract and walked out, though, Ben wouldn't be in trouble with Mr Haskell. Perhaps Ben's deliberately infuriating behaviour was intended to drive her away?

Slowly she walked across the room and sat down on the bed, biting her lower lip. It would be a devious, calculated way of achieving his ends, but the more she thought about it the more likely it seemed. Ben was quite capable of being devious, of deciding to avoid open confrontation with his father and working out that the answer was to taunt her into taking the next plane back to London.

Chloe's face flushed hotly, her eyes had a vivid green glow in them. The swine, she thought, unable to sit still any longer. Getting up she paced to and fro across the room like a caged tigress, trying to work out what to do now. Was she going to react the way Ben planned, pack and go? That would be very satisfactory for Ben, but she was too angry to let him win that easily. Why should she let him have his own way? She hadn't liked the open enjoyment with which he had watched her while he was using that mocking drawl to her. He had been playing with her like a toreador deliberately maddening a bull before he moved in for the kill; he had smiled as he planted his darts, knowing exactly how to torment her, and what made it worse was that his expertise came from all he had learnt about her feelings three years ago. It was love that had taught Ben how to hurt her.

She stopped her angry pacing to stare out of the window at the darkening sky above Venice's terracotta roofs. Evening was coming in quickly now; the air was chilly although it had been such a warm day. Spring was still in its earliest phase and could change at any moment back to winter. Leaning her hot face on the cool glass, Chloe tried to think clearly, but all she could think about was Ben and how much she would like to grab two handfuls of that glossy black hair and pull it hard.

'Damn him,' she said aloud and the words echoed in the quiet room, making her jump at their ferocity. She wasn't going to allow him to manipulate her—she wasn't going to let him stampede her into running away. If she did that, she was admitting how much he could still affect her, she was tacitly admitting she still loved him and in his mood of bitter rejection Ben would take that a triumph.

'I'm staying,' she told herself, flinging the words up at the ceiling as though aiming them at Ben himself, wherever he was in the hotel.

CHAPTER SEVEN

GULLS quarrelled crossly on the white stone balustrade enclosing the hotel terrace, their yellow beaks snapping over the scraps of bread roll which Chloe had just thrown in their direction. She watched, smiling, her eyes half-closed in drowsy contentment. The sunlight was pleasantly warm and she felt relaxed and at easy harmony with the world. For the past three days she had been rehearsing with the band—she had struck a bargain with them with Angelo's friendly help. If the band played for her jazz numbers, she would sing a couple of songs in their style. Although she preferred to sing jazz, she could sing pop just as well—it didn't give her voice the range she wanted, that was all.

The terrace behind her was crowded with hotel staff—everyone was out there eating a cold buffet lunch while Ben gave them a pep talk. Tonight the hotel opened officially with a dinner to which many Venetians had been invited; it was to be a big 'society' occasion with everyone who was anyone in Venice in attendance, and a number of press people on hand to report the festivities. Ben wanted to make sure that nothing went wrong; the hotel had to impress everyone who came tonight.

Chloe had taken her plate of sliced ham and

salad to a table as far away as possible without falling into the Grand Canal over which the terrace looked. During Ben's speech she had watched the vaporetto chugging across to Guidecca, the long island which protruded from behind the Dogana, the famous golden glove whose weather vane figure revolved slowly as the wind blew, on the other side of the canal.

Why shouldn't she explore Guidecca herself that afternoon? she thought. She wouldn't be rehearsing with the band—they wanted to concentrate on the music which had no vocals and Chloe was free to amuse herself. It was such lovely spring weather, a trip on a vaporetto would be fun.

Ben had finished talking, people were drifting away leaving a litter of uneaten food and used plates on the long, damask-draped table which had been laid for the buffet.

'Angelo, what number vaporetto do I catch to go to Guidecca?' Chloe asked, leaning over to where the band were sitting.

'Number five, *numero cinque*,' Angelo supplied readily. He took his self-appointed task as her Italian tutor very seriously and Chloe was already beginning to speak a number of phrases. 'You going there today?' he added questioningly and she nodded.

'I feel just like a boat trip.'

'Okay, but take a scarf—very windy on the vaporetto unless you go down into the cabin. Have fun.' Angelo kissed his fingers to her as she smilingly walked away and she threw him a kiss in reply.

She was in no hurry, she strolled out of the hotel and through the narrow streets to St Mark's which was as crowded as ever with pigeons, tourists, policemen and souvenir salesmen. The four bronze horses on the façade of the Basilica seemed poised to gallop down the square, the green patina of their coats gleaming in the sunlight. Angelo had taken Chloe up to the walkway which ran just below them on a stone-balustraded balcony—at close quarters the horses were even more miraculously life-like. As she turned into the Piazzetta, the smaller square which ran from the Basilica down to the waterfront, she saw the blue sheen of the canal and above it the winged lion of St Mark crouching on a soaring stone column. The wide pavement running along the edge of the lagoon was crowded with vaporetto stops and thronged with people coming and going.

Chloe wandered along, looking at the numbers on the boards above the vaporetto jetties. The curve of the land was crammed with pastel-coloured houses; mostly hotels now, some with restaurants and cafés which opened out on to the Riva degli Schiavoni, this wide pavement along which she was walking. Her gaze followed the line of buildings, her smile wry—there was too much to see, that was the trouble with Venice. A lifetime would be too short to see everything, one had to make a choice and choices were always difficult.

She halted as she reached the stop she wanted and bought a special ticket which gave her a month's travel on any vaporetto wherever she chose to go. It was expensive but in the long run it would save money. Chloe meant to use the vaporetto as often as possible; it was the best way of seeing Venice and the outlying islands, Angelo had told her. You could walk on and off the vaporetto so easily; it was the only public transport, which visited every part of Venice, and there was something romantic about the idea of a bus which moved on water, not roads.

The floating jetty was crowded, she stood on the swaying raft listening to the chatter of Italian voices, waiting for her vaporetto to arrive. When it came, thudding against the tyres hung along the jetty, people crowded to board it. Chloe felt someone behind her, a hand touched her waist, and she stiffened, looking round to rap out an emphatic: '*Va via!*' Angelo had told her that most men would leave her alone if she told them to go away with sufficient force.

It wasn't an Italian stranger, however; it was Ben, his black brows curved sardonically at her. The cross words died on her lips and she went pink with shock.

'What are you doing here?' Ben sounded suspicious and she stammered her reply.

'I ... I'm going over to Guidecca, sight-seeing.'

A large Italian woman with a child clinging to her neck surged forward impatiently, to get past them and board the vaporetto. '*Permesso, per favore,*' she muttered.

'Sorry,' Chloe said, backing. '*Scusi,* I mean.'

She was flustered and rather pink under Ben's sardonic gaze, and wasn't looking where she was going—the next second she skidded on the slippery jetty and toppled forward, unable to stop herself.

Ben leapt forward and grabbed her just before she fell between the jetty and the vaporetto, down into the choppy blue-grey water of the harbour. She was lifted off her feet, his strong arms round her waist, and dropped bodily on to the deck of the vaporetto to the accompaniment of rude laughter from the various men watching, and loud exclamations of concern and dismay from the women.

'*Va bene, signorina?*' one asked her, smiling soothingly, and another clicked her tongue, shaking her head, as though disappointed in Chloe.

Muttering '*Grazie, grazie,*' Chloe stumbled down the steps into the glass-enclosed cabin without looking back at Ben. There were a few empty seats, she slid on to one and hunched into the corner, looking out of the spray-streaked window. She had kept out of Ben's way for the last three days—what evil providence had brought him to the vaporetto stop today? She knew what he had been thinking, she had understood why his brows rose at the sight of her. He suspected her of following him here; what else had that sardonic smile meant? If she protested that she hadn't, that she didn't even want to see him, he wouldn't believe her.

The vaporetto moved off and someone dropped

on to the seat beside her. Chloe went on staring out of the window at the jetty, waiting for a glimpse of Ben's black head among the crowds left behind.

'What are you going to look at on Guidecca?'

She swung round on the seat, her mouth open in a gasp.

'Close your mouth, you look half-witted,' he drawled charmingly and her lips clamped together in a furious line. He lounged back, one arm sliding along the back of the seat, his lean body coolly at ease, but Chloe was far from feeling relaxed—how could she when she was intensely aware of his muscled thigh pressing warmly against her left leg? The slatted wooden seats were admittedly rather narrow, but did Ben have to sit so close?

'Where are you going?' she demanded, shifting away from him.

'To visit friends who live in the Dorsoduro,' Ben said calmly but his blue eyes mocked her agitated withdrawal from all contact.

'What's that?'

'It's the old working-class district of Venice— it's become rather fashionable because the houses are small and easily modernised, the prices of property there have shot up recently.'

The vaporetto began bucking about like an ungainly carthorse as it hit the wake of a larger craft which had just passed them, and Chloe was flung sideways towards Ben, her glossy dark brown hair tossed over her face. She clutched at the nearest object, which turned out to be Ben.

Realising that she had caught hold of his shoulder, she dropped her hands as if he was red hot, muttering: 'Sorry.'

'You'll be safer when you're on dry land,' Ben said drily, then leaned across her suddenly. 'There's San Giorgio Maggiore—we call there first.'

Chloe shrank back against the seat, finding his proximity claustrophobic; she kept her head turned away from him, staring at the tiny island which they were approaching rapidly. The red brick walls of the ancient monastery climbed out of the blue water along one side of the island and she saw the columned white façade of the famous Palladian church in the centre. Chloe had noticed San Giorgio Maggiore each morning at breakfast; the island was often veiled in pearly mist in the early morning. The shimmer of those buildings in the distance had mystery which the island did not have once you were close to it, she thought wryly—and wasn't that just like life? The further you were from anything, the more desirable it seemed, and the reverse was true, too. Distance lent enchantment to any view. What you could have any time you ceased to want.

'I bought a postcard of San Giorgio Maggiore,' she told Ben, turning to give him a glance which tried to assess him and held uncertainty—did she only yearn for Ben because he was out of reach? How real was the way she felt about him?

'To send to your family?' he asked flatly and she knew at once that he was thinking about Jilly—his eyes had darkened and his mouth was tense.

'Yes,' she said defiantly—what was the point of lying about it? She hadn't invited him to come and sit next to her and she couldn't go on avoiding the subject of her family for ever. She might be angry with Jilly now but Chloe still loved her family very much, they were an essential part of her, of her whole life, she could no more cut herself off from them than she could cut herself off from the root of her own nature.

'I suppose your niece will be back from her honeymoon by now,' Ben said curtly, clipping out each word as though he bit it out through his teeth.

'She should be,' admitted Chloe.

Ben's mouth twisted distastefully. 'The man I'm sorry for is her husband—I wouldn't be in his shoes for the world.'

Chloe had thought the same many times since Jilly's wedding—but, contrarily, she didn't agree with him; she gave him an uneasy look and said: 'You know, Jilly was very young—she's grown up a good deal since you last saw her. She's not the same girl.'

'People don't change,' Ben said with brooding harshness and their eyes met in conflict, telling her that Ben hadn't merely been thinking about Jilly. He had been talking about Chloe as much as her niece; it was still Chloe's betrayal that he resented most bitterly.

'Of course they do!' she protested, flinching from the stare of those darkened eyes. 'People change all the time; they do learn from experience, after all—if they didn't we would all still be living in caves and wearing animal skins.'

'However much people may alter on the surface, deep down they tend to react in the same way at any age,' Ben argued impatiently. 'In a crisis Jilly would still lie to save her face—and come to that, she would still lie to boost her own ego. She's basically selfish and shallow, she only sees her own angle.' His gaze challenged her. 'Can you deny that?'

Chloe bit her lip and didn't answer. What could she say? Ben's portrait of Jilly was appallingly accurate, and yet was it?

The vaporetto had docked at San Giorgio and passengers trooped off and on; the waves splashed up over the window while Chloe watched the drops of water trickling down the glass.

'People are never that simple,' she said hesitantly. 'Okay, Jilly is selfish—but she can be very sweet and she's lively and good fun a lot of the time. She's very fond of her parents, she's generous and full of vitality.' She looked at Ben almost pleadingly. 'You paint the picture too black; life is more grey than anything else, and that applies to people, too.'

'Does it apply to you?' Ben asked drily as the vaporetto chugged onward. Chloe stared at the power of his face, laid bare by sunlight; the hard bone structure had a beauty which was entirely masculine, unyielding in its chiselled austerity.

'Of course it does! I'm not perfect, in fact, I'm full of flaws.'

His mouth was crooked. 'Yes.' There was a little silence, then he asked harshly: 'Why did you believe *her*, Chloe? How could you think I'd do that? Make a pass at a girl of that age? Good God, I'd need to be sick in the head—quite apart from the fact that I was in love with you. I didn't even notice that girl. If you were in a room I didn't notice anyone. The only impression she made on me was one of irritation because she was always trying to grab attention. If she'd been my daughter, I'd have slapped her when she interrupted and showed off the way she did.'

'Jilly is spoilt,' Chloe conceded huskily.

'So why did you believe her rather than me?' His hard blue eyes fixed her; she gave a ragged sigh.

'I was in love with you . . .' she began and Ben gave a snarl of denial.

'Oh, no! You couldn't have been! Not if you believed her rather than me!'

'But that's why I believed her—don't you see?' Chloe was whispering now, because several of the other passengers in the vaporetto were staring at them, their attention caught by the vibration of angry emotion. They might not understand English, but in any language the feelings between Chloe and Ben were unmistakably tense. 'I was uncertain about myself, I couldn't believe that you . . .'

'Uncertain about yourself?' he interrupted again. 'I didn't get that impression. You were always so confident, sophisticated; you'd been singing in public for years, how can you pretend you weren't confident?'

'Oh, on stage! Don't you know that one reason why people go into show business is because they're scared?' she flared up. The vaporetto was docking at Guidecca; out of the corner of her eye Chloe saw a long, straight pavement edged with trees, a few shops and the odd hotel. There were few people about, only an old woman in black standing in an open doorway watching the vaporetto turn in to the jetty.

Ben looked disbelievingly at her. 'No, I didn't know that—and I don't believe it either. You need nerve to walk out on a stage and sing in front of an audience—nerve and a supreme sense of self-confidence. You've got both.'

'You need nerves, that's perfectly true, but they aren't the sort you mean. Just before I walk out I almost throw up, every single time. I get goose-bumps, I'm so cold my teeth chatter. We all feel that way. If we didn't, we wouldn't be any good because without that sense of inadequacy, that terrible fear, we wouldn't be so desperate to prove we can do it. It's the fear that drives you out on to that stage.'

The vaporetto was pulling away and turning back towards the main island; Chloe glanced out of the window, suddenly realising that Guidecca was behind them.

'Oh,' she exclaimed, flushing. 'We . . .'

But Ben wasn't listening, he was frowning and watching her face with steady, searching blue eyes.

'I still say you couldn't have cared much for me if you thought me capable of doing what Jilly said I'd done,' he insisted. 'Even if I accept that you were uncertain about *yourself*, that leaves us with the question of what you thought of me. If you'd known anything about me, you wouldn't have believed her, and if you didn't know me well enough to realise she was lying, then you couldn't have loved me.'

Chloe bit her lip unhappily. 'But . . .'

'Admit it, I'm only being logical!'

'Logic hasn't got much to do with love, though, has it?' Chloe sighed, her eyes wandering to the window again. 'Look, you may not have noticed but we're miles past Guidecca now.'

He looked out of the window. 'Damn!' he said, his face surprised and impatient. 'Oh, well, I'll have to get off at the next stop and take a vaporetto back to Guidecca.' He got up, lurching as the vaporetto bounced violently, slowing to stop at a jetty opposite Guidecca. Chloe followed him off the boat, trying to make up her mind what to do—should she go back to the hotel or not?

'Where are we?' she asked Ben, looking around her at the long quay on which they had landed.

'Zattere,' he said. 'Are you going back to Guidecca?'

'No, I think I'll make my way back to St Mark's.' She couldn't face any more of this discussion with Ben; he wouldn't believe her and it was too painful to see the anger in his eyes.

'As you like,' he said shortly. 'You can walk

back, if you like—turn down the street just past that church, the Gesuati church. If you carry straight on, you'll find yourself at the Academy bridge. It's only five or ten minutes walk. On the other side of the bridge follow the black signs to St Mark's—it's a more complicated way than from here to the Academy bridge but it is well sign-posted. You shouldn't have any trouble finding your way. Have you got a map of Venice?'

She pulled one out of her cotton jeans and Ben took it to show her the route. His head was bent close to her face, his hair brushed her cheek, and she watched his face rather than what he was showing her.

'Are you looking?' he asked suddenly, looking up.

She went pink. 'Yes, of course.'

'Liar,' he said in a husky voice, then thrust the map at her. 'Well, get lost then! It's a nice afternoon; it could be fun.'

'Yes, it could,' Chloe said softly, looking at him through lowered lashes, her smile inviting.

Ben looked at her, his face hesitant, irresolute, then suddenly swung away to leap on to another vaporetto which had chugged alongside. He leaned on the deck, staring back at her, as the vaporetto moved off. What was he thinking? Chloe wondered, watching him until he was out of sight, before she turned and began to follow the route back to the hotel.

The afternoon was fine and warm, she didn't hurry and found plenty to see on the way. Before she crossed the bridge she went into the Academy gallery to see some of the finest Venetian paintings; there was far too much to see, she had to skip from room to room, pausing to look at any picture that attracted her without following any particular system. The earlier pictures fascinated her most; there was something so mysterious and awesome about the medieval paintings with their very human faces gazing out of glittering, gilded settings. She found she knew almost nothing about most of the painters; their names weren't familiar and when she left the galleries her head rang with names and sharp impressions of colour and life. She decided to pay some more visits to the Academy; she must find out more about the unknown artists.

While she walked from canvas to canvas she had had to force herself to think about what she was looking at, rather than about Ben. They had at least talked today; for the first time there had been a flimsy contact between them which was not a bitter conflict. She felt faintly optimistic; yet it would be stupid to hope, wouldn't it? Ben had made it clear that he still found her attractive, but that didn't mean much. He didn't like her. That was what counted. Chloe didn't want him to touch her while he looked at her with such hostility; she might start to hate herself if she was weak enough to give in to her own need for Ben, in his present mood.

After she had crossed the wooden Academy bridge, she slowly found her way through the alleys and squares beyond it, past the pale pink

church of San Vidal, the tall balconied Palazzo
Morosini, along paved streets full of shadow and
open spaces full of sunlight, until she got into the
winding alleys behind the hotel.

Angelo came out of a camera shop as she was
passing it and Chloe stopped, smiling.

'Hi, had a good day?' he asked, joining her.

'I've seen quite a bit of Venice, anyway,' Chloe
compromised. She wasn't so sure it had been a
good day; some of it she had enjoyed but at times
she had wished she was somewhere else.

They walked on together and Angelo pointed
out the small square in which you could buy the
hand-made masks. 'Oh, I must get one!' Chloe
hurried towards the double row of stalls, her eye
caught by the gleam of gold and silver masks—a
gilded lion's head, a silver goat's head with
twisting, shimmering horns, the green glass eyes
of a tiger staring down at you from a striped and
terrifying head. There was enormous variety, she
didn't know which to choose, moving from stall
to stall to look at owl masks made of soft grey
feathers, the white face of a clown, sinister black
half-masks made of leather. Angelo indulgently
translated the prices and chatted to the young
students selling their wares.

In the end Chloe bought herself a pink mask
made of delicate feathers; it only covered half her
face but when her eyes gazed through the slanted
openings she looked totally unfamiliar, a stranger
even to herself. Angelo talked her into buying a
black lace mantilla cape in traditional design and
a black tricorne hat with a large silk rosette on

one side. She put them all on and gazed at herself in the small hand mirror, smiling.

'Gorgeous!'

'*Si, si,*' Angelo agreed, laughing. 'You look *meravigliosa*! Wonderful!'

'I didn't mean me—I meant the mask and mantilla!' she protested, taking them off and allowing the young student to pack them into a carrier bag for her. 'Now I can enjoy the carnival, when it begins,' she told Angelo.

'Why don't you hire a costume, too?' suggested Angelo as they walked back. 'A friend of mine runs a shop where you could get a special price— he'll do it as a favour for me, okay?'

Chloe allowed herself to be persuaded and spent an enchanted hour going through all the ravishing costumes. Angelo wanted her to choose a harem girl's outfit but Chloe giggled, refusing to do anything of the kind, although she couldn't resist trying it on and enjoyed the wolf-whistle she got from the young man running the shop.

'Take it, take it,' begged Angelo, eyes gleaming. 'You see, most girls, they wouldn't look good in it but you . . . you have the figure.' He bunched his fingers together and kissed them and Chloe backed into the fitting room, shaking her head and laughing. It was far too flimsy and revealing; she couldn't see herself walking around the Venice streets in that.

She chose what she had really known she wanted as soon as she came into the shop; a costume which perfectly matched her mask and black lace cape. It was the traditional Venetian

costume for women; full-skirted pink brocade
with a tight waist, low neckline and long sleeves
ending in a flurry of ruffled silk, in the
eighteenth-century style which was most popular
for the carnival. The shop-owner produced a fan
which matched it and Chloe paraded up and
down, fluttering her fan and gazing at the two
young men over it, her eyes gleaming through the
feathered mask. She didn't need to ask them how
she looked—their faces were eloquent enough.

Angelo helped her to carry her various
packages back to the hotel. The streets grew more
crowded every day, she noticed. Tourists were
flooding into Venice for the Carnival festivities;
most of which she would miss because she would
be singing every night.

'The problem is—when am I going to be able
to wear my costume?' she said mournfully to
Angelo who grinned.

'They dance in the square until midnight on
most evenings during the Carnival—we'll go out
to join in the fun when we've finished playing.
You'll come with us, okay? The big night is
Mardi Gras, we're having a dance at the hotel
that night—didn't you hear the boss tell us so this
morning? I thought you weren't listening to him;
you were day-dreaming, right?'

'I'm afraid so,' Chloe admitted, grimacing. She
hadn't heard what Ben said because she had been
too busy listening to the deep notes of his voice
and weaving them into daydreams so vivid that
she couldn't possibly tell Angelo about them.

'Well, okay, he said we would have a carnival

ball, starting at eleven o'clock, to give the guests time to go out, see the fun in the streets, and get back to dance here. They'll be dancing in St Mark's square, but you can't sit down anywhere or have a drink because the crowds are too big. There is more room at the hotel. So you can wear your costume for Mardi Gras; why not sing in it? Sound good?'

'Sounds great,' Chloe said excitedly. She couldn't wait to see Ben's face when he saw her in the costume.

That night as she changed into the black silk dress she would be wearing for the grand opening of the hotel, she began to get that old, familiar sick tension in the stomach, the waves of doubt and self-questioning. What if her voice went? She put a hand to her throat, convinced suddenly that she was getting a sore throat. She couldn't swallow, her mouth was dry, there was a prickling irritation at the back of her throat. Her voice would break, she wouldn't be able to reach the high notes. She hurriedly gargled, drank some water, then felt the clutch of nausea, her stomach lurching violently. God, she was going to be sick. She ran into the bathroom, ashen and sweating.

All sorts of nightmare visions flashed through her mind—what if she forgot the words of her songs? What if the band were out of step with her? People might laugh. At once she saw rows of faces, a battery of mocking eyes staring at her, and she became paralysed with fear, her knees knocking. She couldn't go down—her legs wouldn't carry her, she knew she wasn't going to be able to sing.

Ben would be there; among all those strangers. He would see her make a fool of herself; he would smile or look pityingly at her. She couldn't bear it. She looked at her reflection with distaste; why had she decided to wear this dress, anyway? She hated slinky black dresses; what on earth had possessed her to buy one with a slit at each side which fell back when she walked, revealing her legs up to the thigh? God, it was horrible, she hated the dress. The neckline was too low, there was too much of her on display, and what the sleek black dress did cover it somehow made just as blatant—the silky material clung to her figure as though it was her outer skin and she was naked. Some women might be able to wear sophisticated dresses like this one, but she flinched from her own reflection. She had bought it in a mood of reckless daring, but now she was sober and nervous. She didn't have the courage to project the sophisticated sex appeal the dress suggested—what had made her think she could do it?

The 'phone rang and she jumped about ten feet in the air. Who was that? She couldn't move, staring bolt-eyed, at the 'phone while it rang insistently making her nerves go crazy. At last she leant over and grabbed for it with a shaking hand.

'Hallo?' she croaked into the wrong end and heard a squawking sound from the earpiece. She fumbled with the receiver and managed to get her lips to the mouthpiece. 'Hallo?' she tried again.

'Are you okay?' It was Ben, sounding concerned and anxious.

'Oh ... f ... fine ...' she said rustily, surprised her voice worked at all.

'Angelo asked me to ring—you should be down here, you're on in five minutes.' There was a pause, then he said: 'Your voice sounds odd—don't tell me you've got a sore throat?'

'No, I'm okay,' Chloe said, crossing her fingers behind her back although as he couldn't see her there was no need to hide the gesture.

There was a little silence, then Ben said quietly: 'Nervous?'

'Do I sound nervous?' she asked, giving a totally unconvincing laugh.

'Yes,' Ben said and she wailed.

'God, I'm petrified!'

'Shall I come up?'

'No, yes, no,' she babbled, took a long breath and said more calmly: 'No, I'm coming now, I'll be there in one minute.'

She was about to replace the 'phone when he said: 'I love your voice, you're a marvellous singer,' then he hung up too rapidly for her to be able to answer him. She put down the receiver slowly. That had been nice of him; he had been kind and she was grateful for that kindness, it was like standing in front of a warm fire when you're shivering. Smiling, she walked firmly to the door.

She never knew how she got down to the

restaurant or walked out on to the stage when Angelo introduced her, she had no recollection later of starting to sing her first song. She surfaced again to realisation halfway through it as she let her whole voice out and the audience sat up as though a bomb had just gone off. Chloe's eyes cleared and she saw Ben at the far back of the room, a lean, tanned man in formal black evening dress, his arms folded as he listened to her, his face in shadow. Chloe sang a blues song, full of brooding passion, her shapely body generously curved as it swayed in front of the mike, her pale throat vibrating with the music she was making, she was pouring everything she was into that sound, the room shuddered in the force of it.

Her last note hung for a long time on the still air, quivering, poignant. Nobody moved, people hardly seemed to breath. There was a silence that seemed to last for ever, then a storm of applause broke out and Chloe almost winced in the first shock of it. People whistled, stamped, banged their hands on the tables—she laughed, looking round at Angelo and the band, who were grinning ear to ear. They clapped her, hands raised high, and she turned to clap back at them, then gestured to them, smiling at the audience. After the tension had snapped she was euphoric, elated, so high she felt she could sail out of the window and float like a crazy kite above the city. There wasn't a drug to touch it—nothing else could give you that kick.

When she walked off the stage, people spoke to

her, men caught her hand, women smiled; it took her a long time to get out of the room and she couldn't go to bed after that. She had to get some air, she was so hot she was burning up. She went out of the swing doors into the warm Venetian night. The little square behind the hotel was lit with moonlight. She gazed up at the bank walls running around all four sides of it and then up at the white-faced moon.

She breathed in deeply, her body slowly calming to a quieter beat. It had been quite a day.

She wandered across the square, remembering Ben's face before she began to sing. When she had finished singing Ben had vanished from the back of the room; even while she was taking her bows she had noticed his absence. She had looked for him, puzzled, slightly hurt. Why had he left?

It wasn't until she became aware of the darkness around her that she realised she had turned out of the moonlit square into a narrow, unlit alley. She was about to turn back when she heard a footstep close behind her. Her head swung, she saw a shape in the shadows, and in a surge of alarm began to hurry along the alley to a lighted area from which she could hear voices, echoing across the canal with that odd distance of sounds heard at night across water. The footsteps behind her quickened, too, she heard the soft slap of soles on the pavement, then a hand shot out and grabbed her.

Chloe screamed.

'What the hell are you doing?' Ben asked; his voice hard, impatient, very familiar.

Chloe sagged, her heart thudding in shock. 'Oh, it's you!'

His face glowered down at her. 'Yes, it is, luckily for you—it might easily have been someone more dangerous!'

'I doubt it,' Chloe said, suddenly reckless after the euphoria of her triumph a few moments ago.

'And you can cut that out,' Ben said sharply. 'I'm being serious! Don't you know it isn't safe to wander around a strange city at night? Especially in a dress like that?'

Her veins ran with heat at the way he had said that, but she protested weakly: 'Angelo told me Venice was the safest city in Italy!'

'In that dress you wouldn't be safe with any man anywhere,' Ben informed her through his teeth. Chloe's heart missed another beat.

'Except you,' she prompted softly, watching him and saw his eyes glitter.

'Me least of all,' he said, his voice deep and rough, and the hand gripping her wrist slid slowly up her bare arm, sending a shudder of desire through her.

Chloe swayed helplessly, her body molten with passion and Ben stared at the parted pink lips she raised towards him. She heard his breathing; harsh, uneven, like the sound of a drowning man fighting for air.

'I should have sent you packing that first day,' he muttered. His hand slid down her bare back and her silk-clad body moved restlessly against him—why didn't he kiss her? She knew he wanted to; he couldn't hide that look in his eyes, they were brilliant with desire.

'No, Chloe,' he said fiercely, but she felt his fingers trembling on her skin and she knew he wanted her. 'I won't let a woman make a fool of me twice,' he said, and she ran her arms around his neck and clasped his nape.

'Ben, listen . . .'

'No, I don't want to hear what you have to say. We're going back to the hotel and from now on you're only to go out at night if you're with a party of other people, is that understood?' But he hadn't thrust her arms down and he wasn't pushing her away, she felt the tremor of aroused sensuality in his body as she clung to him. He hadn't taken his eyes off her mouth; she sensed that in his imagination he had already kissed it, he breathed faster and faster until he suddenly pulled away from her, turned on his heel and began to walk away, one hand fastening round her wrist to pull her after him.

When they were back in the lighted hotel Ben didn't look at her again. 'Goodnight,' he muttered, walking away, and Chloe slowly went over to the lift. She was very cold now, shaky and close to tears. For a minute she had been sure Ben was going to hold her, kiss her, but he was even more stubborn than she had known. The stone wall of his resentment over the past was not that easy to crack; how did you break through a barrier like that? Chloe lay awake for two hours trying to work that out; she fell asleep with the problem unresolved.

CHAPTER EIGHT

ON the night of Mardi Gras, you couldn't walk through St Mark's square, it was too crowded—you had to shuffle along the arcades on either side of it, in a constantly flowing stream of bodies jammed so close they carried you with them even if you didn't want to go. It could have been frightening, if the crowd hadn't been so good-tempered. In the time it took Angelo and Chloe to cover half of the square, she had been kissed a dozen times—once by a cardinal, twice by owls and several times by Superman. The costumes everyone was wearing stunned her by their variety—photographers were popping up all over the place to get shots of some of the best.

'This way!' Angelo yanked her sideways down the steps into the square and she almost toppled over as her wide skirts flared.

Several laughing young men leapt to catch her, one offered her a glass of wine, another snatched a kiss; they both had painted faces in bold punk colours, zigzags of green on their foreheads and orange and red lines on their cheeks.

'*Permesso*,' Angelo said coldly, retrieving her.

'*Scusi, scusi,*' bowed the young men.

'*Non importa,*' Chloe soothed them, smiling, and they cheered up and danced away to find other amusement. 'Do they paint their faces themselves or get their girlfriends to do it?' Chloe asked Angelo, who shrugged.

'Some of the art students charge a hundred lire to paint your face; it is cheaper than one of the *paper maché* masks—the colours wash off. Okay, now we dance?'

The music was being relayed around the square by loudspeakers fixed on pillars. On the garishly lit stage, the band played with manic energy; the singer leaping about in tight black leather pants and a flame-red Tee-shirt, his acrobatics bringing screams of excitement from the girls closest to the stage. Angelo waved and the band noticed him and grinned, waving back and yelling something in Italian.

'You know them?' Chloe asked.

'Sure, I work with them once, but my face doesn't fit, you know? They're great guys, but I don't like their music—for me, I mean. I want to play different stuff.'

He was wearing a page-boy's outfit of the same period as her own costume; a handsome plum-coloured coat, a silver-embroidered waistcoat and a casually tied white neck cloth. He had a black mask and a white wig, but he had pushed his mask back across his head because he said he was too hot inside it.

Dancing wasn't easy in the packed square; Angelo guided her over to one of the open-air cafés after half an hour and they grabbed two chairs as the occupants got up to leave. Dancers kept circling the café, watching for a chance to get a table, you had to be quick, or you lost your opportunity.

The waiter didn't arrive for ten minutes, but that didn't matter—Chloe was far from bored, watching the costumes and masks on the revolving dancers who flowed past. Above the square the deep blue night sky was pricked with stars; the moon hung high above them like a white balloon. The façade of St Mark's was spotlit, the gold mosaics glittering above the heads of the people flowing past the Basilica.

'When we've drunk our lemonade, why don't we go and watch the fireworks being let off?' suggested Angelo. 'They are going to use a raft in the middle of the bay. From the Riva degli Schiavoni we'll get a perfect view.'

They weren't the only people to get that idea— as they began forcing a passage through the crowd they found themselves engulfed in a stampede towards the Piazzetta, the smaller square leading at right angles from the large Piazza down to the waterfront on the Riva degli Schiavoni. Suddenly Chloe was swept away from Angelo and saw his hand waving desperately as she peered back across the heads of the people nearest to her. He called something she didn't catch and she smiled a reassurance to him, waving her own hand. She wasn't really alarmed, she knew exactly where she was and how to get back to the hotel. The crowd was still cheerful, even if it was uncomfortable to be pushed and prodded from all sides. Chloe began to feel suffocated and she was afraid her lovely dress would get torn; people were treading on the hem of the skirt as they tried to force a way past her.

She edged sideways gradually and managed to get up on to the arcade running along the right hand side of the square. From up there she saw Angelo's silver wig, the mask on the top of his head, his plum coat and the worried look on his face as he tried to catch sight of her in the throng, then the crowd surged round the corner and Angelo vanished with it.

Chloe leaned on a pillar, fanning herself. She was so hot that she put a hand up to her feather mask, meaning to pull it off. A tall man in a black velvet jacket and black leather mask materialised in front of her, his eyes glittering through the slanted eye holes in his mask. She knew him at once; there couldn't be two men with that long, arrogant nose; that hard, cynical mouth. In his costume Ben looked oddly sinister, he radiated menace even when he half smiled.

'*Gradisce a ballare?*' he asked in deep Italian and she stared incredulously. He hadn't recognised her! She was so stunned that she didn't answer him, and, presumably thinking that she hadn't understood him he gestured to the crowd which was still dancing to the band and then held out his hand to her, giving a low bow.

Chloe slowly put her hand into his and let him lead her down from the arcade. There was far more room to dance in the square now that half the crowd had rushed off to see the fireworks. Ben put his arm around her waist and drew her close, she laid a hand on his wide shoulder and they moved off in silence. The band was playing an Italian ballad, an old song which had once been very popular; it had a sweet rhythmic beat which made it easy to dance to.

Ben didn't speak, neither did Chloe. She was swaying in his arms, her eyes lowered, wondering how long it would take him to realise who he was holding. Through her lashes she could just see the hard edge of his profile below the sinister mask; his mouth and jawline radiated that stubborn refusal to bend that was keeping them apart.

He glanced down at her; behind their masks they were no more strangers than they were unmasked. What did she know about him, anyway? All the little things; that he liked hard centred chocolates and playing squash, enjoyed action films and listened to both jazz and opera, drove fast and became impatient when he had to wait for anything, burnt up energy as if he had tons to spare, insisted on having things done his way and wasn't above using coercion if necessary. That was just the surface reality of Ben; what was underneath it, was there another Ben?

Her full skirts floated around her feet as they danced, she was hot under the delicate pink mask, but she couldn't take it off. She deliberately put her cheek against Ben's face, his skin was as heated as her own.

'Those feathers tickle,' he said, his arm tightening on her waist.

She smiled and her head turned slightly, her smiling lips touched his cheek. She felt the quiver that ran through his face, then he too turned his head and his mouth searched for hers with an urgency that made her head swim. They went on dancing, but the kiss deepened, Ben put both his arms around her and his whole body pressed tautly against her; the hand in the small of her back forcing her even closer. Sighing and yielding, she ran her arms around his neck and clenched her hands in his thick hair, holding his head down. Wolf whistles and ribald comments came from all around them, but neither of them took any notice. They were dancing and making love at the same time, hands and bodies restless with passion; masked and in the dark there was no need to pretend or deny the emotions they hid in daylight. They were briefly free, uninhibited by the past or old resentments—it didn't matter if they knew each other or were strangers.

Then Chloe stumbled over a rough paving stone, Ben lifted his head, she looked up at him and was abruptly flung back into the real world and the real masks they wore in public. She heard the crack of a firework being exploded; the sky blossomed with bright colour, dousing the light of the stars for a second, and Ben's eyes gleamed down at her through the black leather mask.

He knows who I am, she thought; why doesn't he say anything? Was that malice or mockery in his eyes?

She pushed him away and ran; grabbing her skirts and fleeing before Ben could catch up with her. She weaved through the other dancers who had halted to stare upwards at the falling shower of coloured stars. Was Ben following her? She made it to the edge of the square without being caught, glanced back before she turned out into the alley beyond, and could only see the confused tangle of people in their many-coloured costumes. There was no sign of Ben. Perhaps he hadn't recognised her, perhaps he thought he had been dancing with a stranger? Chloe didn't like that thought much; angrily she walked fast along the streets to the hotel, dodging through the other passers-by flowing in and out of St Mark's square. There were still plenty of people around even in this quieter area of the city.

She went straight up to her room and pulled off her mask in the lift; dangling it from her wrist as she walked along the corridor. A green frog flapped past her; laughing eyes peering out of the bulbous *papier mache* mask. She couldn't even tell whether it was a woman or a man behind the quilted green costume. The black rubber webbed feet enforced a shuffling movement on the human being inside them.

'*Ciao!*' Chloe said, smiling.

'*Ciao!*' said the frog.

How was it to dance with those feet? wondered Chloe as she let herself into her room. She went into the bathroom and washed her hot face before she dried it again and re-applied her make-up. She had worn a blue dress when she sang earlier but she had promised Angelo and the band that she would wear her costume at the ball which was being held at the hotel later that night. She was going to sing again, this time Angelo wanted her to sing a ballad, one of the sweet, romantic love songs so popular in Italy. She had spent some time memorising the Italian words; it wasn't a song she had ever heard in England.

Had Ben known it was her? She put on her mask again and stared at her reflection, which instantly became unfamiliar—odd what a difference the mask made!

She looked at her clock; it was half-past ten. She had half-an-hour before she had to appear downstairs to sing with the band. She could go down to the bar but she was afraid of running into Ben. She took off her mask again and lifted the phone to ring Room Service and ask them to send up some ice-cream and a cool drink. She was unbearably over-heated after the dancing and that hurried return to the hotel.

She only had to wait ten minutes for her drink, most of the hotel guests were out in the city, watching the fireworks or dancing in the square. Room Service wasn't overworked for the moment but the young waiter who brought her tray told her gloomily that they expected a big rush any minute now as people came back to the hotel for the ball.

When he had left, Chloe carefully sat down on the brocade couch in her room and sipped her drink. She couldn't eat all of the Neapolitan ice-cream; they had sent up an enormous portion, and soft whipped cream decorated the globes of chocolate, strawberry and vanilla ice. She had to scoop it all off and pile it in a saucer before she ate any of the ice-cream, she couldn't even imagine how many calories were in that lot.

At eleven o'clock precisely she went back

downstairs. The staff had spent a long time decorating the ballroom, which was intended to double as a conference chamber; coloured streamers hung from the ceiling, balloons and Italian flags floated between them and the Murano chandeliers glittered and sparkled in the centre of the room. Along the walls were draped twisted ribbons of gleaming coloured foil; red, green and silver, the Italian colours. Below them tables had been arranged, each with four or six chairs around them, while the vast area of parquet was left clear for dancing. The staff were in costume, too; the men dressed in eighteenth century livery, velvet coats and knee-breeches in the same plum-colour that Angelo was wearing. The girls wore peasant dress; white ruffled blouses and black pinafores with full skirts.

The band were tuning their instruments and looked up with smiles as she joined them. 'Where did you get to?' Angelo demanded. 'Did you see the fireworks? Great, huh?'

'I didn't see them, I came back here when we got lost.'

'That's a pity—you really missed something,' Angelo said. 'Some pretty big rockets; many colours. You should have heard the crowd go "ooh". It was good fun.'

'It was the crowd I was worried about—there were too many people heading to the Riva to watch the fireworks being let off. I was afraid of being knocked over.'

'Oh, they were okay,' Angelo said blithely. 'Carnival crowds are no trouble.'

'You're not a woman!' Chloe contested, rubbing her bottom ruefully. 'I'm black and blue from being pinched.'

The band roared with laughter and she eyed them sternly.

'I don't think it's funny! I felt like someone fighting off a whole flock of octopus—or should it be a school of octopuses?'

Angelo gave a smiling shrug. 'Never mind—is a compliment, you know?'

'A what?'

'Sure, you have a cute behind, that's all it means.'

'So do you,' Chloe told him and the band shrieked. 'Do they pinch yours?' she enquired as Angelo went pink.

'They better not!' He offered to punch Georgio when his friend made pinching movements towards him. 'Get off, *capisce*?'

The guests were arriving, filtering into the ballroom in small groups and being shown to tables by the liveried footmen. The band separated and a moment later began to play. Chloe slipped off to one side until she was called to sing. She saw Ben stroll into the room; he was still in his costume although he had shed his black mask. Her throat began to pulse with nervous anticipation as he glanced around— would she be able to tell whether he had recognised her or not when they danced in the square? His cool gaze drifted over her, she watched intently, but he didn't give a thing away.

The lights were dimmed, Ben came up on to

the platform and made a brief speech introducing
the band and pleading with guests to start
dancing, then he vanished again and a few
couples drifted on to the floor. Waiters were
circulating, serving drinks and snacks of crisps,
tiny hors d'oeuvres or bowls of nuts. Chloe saw
Ben joining some people at a table close to the
platform. He talked for a while, then he led one
of the girls out on to the floor to dance.

Chloe watched, glad her pink mask hid her
expression. Ben was smiling down at the girl in
his arms, and she looked entranced. Chloe
recognised the way Ben was talking; that charm
had been shown to her once, long ago. She hadn't
seen much evidence of it lately.

Angelo turned and gestured to her. She went
up on to the platform again as the band ended
that number with a roll of drums. The dancers
went back to their tables. Angelo talked huskily
into his mike, introducing Chloe. There was a
rustle of applause, then she began to sing. Her
second number was a funny, sophisticated little
song for which she chose to come down from the
platform and stroll among the tables, singing to
the guests. That caused a lot of laughter,
especially when she kissed her hand to one of the
older men who promptly threw her a red
carnation from his buttonhole.

When she reached the table at which Ben sat
she felt the cool warning of his stare telling her
not to play any games with him, but Chloe was in
a reckless mood tonight. She swayed sideways
and sat on his knee. The audience loved it. Ben

was not amused. Leaning back against his shoulder, Chloe sang softly, one hand ruffling his hair. Her eyes flirted. Ben regarded her with narrow-eyed impassivity. She spread her fan and looked at him over the top of it, then sang a particularly naughty line in the song before covering her whole face as though abashed. The audience chuckled and clapped.

Ben's hand suddenly shot out and ran round her throat, clasping her nape and lifting her up towards him as if she was a doll. He held her, helpless, while he kissed her. The applause was deafening. Under cover of it, Ben muttered: 'Now, that is enough—go back on stage.'

Their eyes were inches apart. 'Kiss me again first,' Chloe said smokily, smiling.

'Don't provoke me,' Ben said, still pretending to look calm.

'Into what?' she asked, opening her eyes wide.

'You'll find out,' he promised.

'I can't wait.' Her lashes fluttered at him. Ben grabbed her fan and almost in the same movement twisted her round on his knee so that she was face down across it. She felt the light slap of the fan across her bottom and heard the audience's delighted reaction, then she was on her feet again. Ben rose and handed her back the fan with a bow. Chloe instinctively opened the fan and fanned herself rapidly to cover her flushed cheeks. Ben sat down again, staring at her mockingly as she turned away to walk back on stage.

Angelo and the band were grinning, ear to ear.

'Great, terrific!' they hissed at her as she rejoined them.

She sang the final chorus of the song, the whole audience joining in, and then curtsied as the thunderous applause broke out.

'You were wonderful,' Angelo said, rising to kiss her hand with charming, Latin gallantry. 'We ought to get you and the boss to do that little act every time. It worked like a charm. You didn't say you had worked out a routine with him. Very sneaky!'

Flushed, Chloe shrugged, laughing. She sang two more songs during the next hour but the applause was never so loud again, but then she didn't involve Ben in her act again—that might be pushing him too far. When she had finished singing she danced with a few of the guests, men introduced to her by Ben; they were all Venetians, and, she suspected, quite important. Ben's manner to them was friendly and distinctly careful. They had asked to meet her and Ben had been obliged to bring her over to their table. From his cool face, you would never guess that there was anything between himself and Chloe other than an employer-employee relationship, yet once or twice Chloe caught an icy sparkle in his blue eyes when he glanced at her. She got the feeling she wouldn't escape scot free after her teasing provocation earlier. She hoped Ben wasn't planning some sort of repercussion.

She slept very well that night; it had been an exhausting day followed by an even more eventful evening. She woke up rather late and felt sleepy as she stumbled into the shower, but the sting of the water brought her fully awake and by the time she had dressed in a cool, lemon top and cotton pants of the same colour, she was feeling hungry and in need of some strong coffee.

Angelo was at the breakfast table, sipping black coffee and eating parma ham with chunks of yellow melon. He raised a lacklustre hand.

'Hi.'

'You look very down,' Chloe said, helping herself to some melon. 'Headache?'

He groaned. 'I wish I was dead.'

'That can be arranged,' she promised, smiling, and he produced a weak grin. 'Too much Chianti, last night?' asked Chloe more sympathetically and he nodded, then put a hand to his head as though afraid it might fall off any minute.

'Have some more coffee,' Chloe offered, pouring herself a cup.

While she ate her melon and then a croissant, Angelo brooded on his health, his head propped up on one hand. Chloe was just drinking her second cup of coffee when Ben appeared, the sunlight gleaming on his thick black hair.

The waiters all began to look very busy and efficient, the restaurant manager hurried to meet him with a welcoming smile, Angelo sat up and poured himself another cup of black coffee with a hand he tried to hold steady.

Ben detached himself from the manager and came over to their table, meeting Chloe's wary eyes with a blank expression.

'I'd like a word,' he drawled. 'In my office. As

soon as you've finished.' He turned to look at
Angelo who gazed back like a rabbit caught in
headlights. 'You and your band were very good
last night. I had a number of compliments. Well
done.'

'*Grazie, grazie,*' Angelo sighed with relief, but
Ben was already striding away and as soon as he
had gone Angelo subsided with a groan. 'He is
too much,' he moaned at the table cloth. '*Molto*
terrible!'

'*Molto* rat, you mean,' Chloe said, swallowing
the last of her coffee and almost burning her
mouth.

Angelo thought that was very funny; he was
still laughing as she left the restaurant. Chloe
stood outside Ben's office, screwing up her nerve
before she knocked on the door. He was going to
turn nasty about the way she had behaved last
night, she knew that. She shouldn't have done it;
it had been a crazy impulse and she regretted it
now. She had tweaked the lion's tail and now she
might find herself being eaten alive and it would
all be her own fault.

She tapped on the office door. Ben said curtly:
'Come in,' and when she sidled into the office he
leaned back in the chair behind the desk, eyeing
her with dangerous urbanity.

'Close the door and sit down,' he said, his tone
silky, the voice that of a spider inviting a fly to
drop in for a snack.

The office seemed to swell to enormous
proportions; Chloe trekked across it feeling very
small and isolated. If she had known Ben was

going to hold a post mortem on her behaviour last night, she wouldn't have put on casual clothes like the pretty lemon cotton outfit. She would have worn something elegant and classy; something to give her confidence a lift and make her feel coolly untouchable. Ben watched her imperturbably until she fell into a chair and faced him across the desk, dragging an unconvincing smile into her face.

'Sorry about last night,' she babbled, hoping to pre-empt his strike and disarm him in advance. 'It was the champagne! I never have been able to drink more than two glasses of wine, and it went to my head.'

'I thought something had!' Ben drawled and she went bright pink under his sardonic stare. Was he hinting at the way they had kissed as they danced in the square? She couldn't tell from those cool blue eyes; Ben hid his secret thoughts.

'It seemed like a good idea to bring you into the act,' she improvised hastily. 'I didn't think you'd mind, it was all playful.'

Ben got up and she tensed, watching him with nervous eyes as he strolled around the desk and leaned against the edge of it, his arms folded, eyeing her in a fashion she found distinctly unnerving. He's going to tell me to pack up and fly home, she guessed. She didn't want to go, she didn't want to leave him. He might still scowl at her, he might show hostility at times, but she kept getting glimpses of the Ben she loved, and if she left now she might never get another chance to reach him.

'Playful, was it?' he asked, raising one brow.

Chloe tried to look blandly innocent. 'All part of the act, getting the audience to join in helps,' she murmured.

Ben leaned down very close, his nose two inches from hers. Chloe tried not to flinch or back away.

'You're a phoney!' Ben said abruptly and Chloe's eyes widened in shock and hurt surprise. She looked down hurriedly to hide the instinctive sting of tears she tried to hold back. How could he say that to her? He must despise her to accuse her of such a thing; she had begun to hope she was making him forget the past but obviously Ben hadn't forgotten a thing, he still hated her.

CHAPTER NINE

'A COMPLETE and utter fake! Aren't you?' Ben said, inviting her to condemn herself.

Chloe stayed stubbornly silent, her eyes lowered. He caught her chin between firm fingers and tilted her head until she had to look at him; she blinked hurriedly to clear the tears from her lashes.

'Look at me,' Ben said with soft menace.

She looked reluctantly into the ice-blue eyes and found the enlarged black pupils glowing hypnotically. Her heart began banging inside her chest, like the drum in a carnival procession, announcing happiness to come, but she couldn't believe what she thought she saw.

'You put on such a big act,' Ben mocked. 'So sophisticated, so sure of yourself; quite a performance. The way you come on anyone would think you never had a single doubt about yourself. But the whole thing is phoney, isn't it? You aren't certain about anything.'

'I'm human,' she countered, still uncertain of him. 'What did you think I was?'

'God knows, I suppose I had some wild dream of the perfect woman—and I projected it on to you, I tried to make you fit the blueprint I had in my head. Nobody sees straight when they fall in love; nothing is real. We're all on our best behaviour, trying to impress, papering over the cracks in our characters like somebody decorating a house before they try to sell it. I knew I had faults—I didn't want you to have any.'

'That's why I wasn't sure if you could have made a pass at Jilly,' Chloe said urgently. 'I wasn't sure about anything, I didn't know enough about you and I got confused and hurt.'

'So did I,' Ben said with a depth that made her flinch.

'I'm sorry, Ben, I'm so sorry—I wish . . .'

'Don't,' he said harshly. 'Wishing is pointless. We have to look at what we have and what we really are—and I'm as much of a fake as you are. I've been busy pretending ever since I saw you again outside my house. I don't know who the hell I thought I was kidding. I just couldn't bring myself to admit how much you still meant to me.'

Chloe trembled with a pleasure so intense it was more like pain, and Ben watched her face, his eyes dark.

'Don't pretend to be amazed,' he said drily. 'You knew, didn't you? That's why you came to Venice. I suppose my father knew, too—and set the whole thing up behind my back. I was furious with him for interfering in my life, but he was right, damn him. I must have given myself away somehow—and I thought I was playing it so cool, showing a real poker face, when all the time the way I felt about you must have been written in letters ten feet high for everyone to see.'

'No, no, I wish it had been,' Chloe said shakily, smiling. 'I was miserable, wondering if

I'd been mistaken, feeling a fool. One minute I thought you might still care, the next I was convinced you hated the sight of me.'

Ben lifted her out of the chair, his hands urgent. 'Don't try to pull the wool over my eyes,' he said with husky impatience. 'You knew very well that I found it hard to keep my hands off you.' He looked at her mouth with half-closed eyes, breathing audibly, then he was kissing her with a ruthless insistence that she didn't seem to mind at all. She yielded meekly, her body soft and pliant as it swayed against him. Her arms went round his neck, one hand closing in his thick black hair, the other clasping his throat and feeling the drive of his blood under her fingers, and Ben's arms locked on her as if she was making sure she couldn't break free ever again.

When Ben finally released her mouth neither of them could breathe very well for a minute; they leaned on each other, shuddering, eyes closed, Ben's cheek rubbing against hers.

'I'm not sure I know you very well, even now,' Ben whispered. 'I only know one thing for certain—I want you, whoever you are. I love you, in spite of myself. I tried hard to talk myself out of love but you're under my skin, I can't pry you out. When you smile at me I feel happy. I missed you badly. Every year I made a resolution that I wouldn't think about you and every year I broke it, you wouldn't stay out of my head. I'm not even certain why I feel the way I do. You aren't beautiful but when I see you, I always think you are. I like the way your face is arranged, I like the way you laugh, I like the way your mind works, even if I don't always understand it.'

Chloe lazily turned her head to let her lips brush his mouth and felt the quick response.

'Say it,' Ben whispered, and she didn't pretend not to know what he meant.

'I love you,' she said huskily. 'You know that— why else would I follow you to Venice?'

He smiled, eyes amused. 'I couldn't believe it when I got back from London and heard you were arriving, you know. That really shook me.'

Chloe grimaced. 'Did you feel hunted?'

'I'm not sure what I felt—I told myself I was furious, but that wasn't entirely true.' He sat down in the chair she had been using and pulled her down on to his lap. Chloe curved close to him, her head against his arm, and he smiled down into her eyes. 'Oh, I was still angry with you—but the way I felt was more complicated than that. I found it exciting to have you around, I wanted to see you. Even our quarrels made me feel high. Life had been pretty grey since I said goodbye to you; suddenly my adrenalin was running again, and if I'd been honest I'd have admitted that it was because I was seeing you.' He ran a hand gently over her hair and down her throat, and Chloe's mouth went dry at the look in his eyes. Desire flared between them although they weren't even kissing; her face burnt and she looked down.

'I thought you might despise me for chasing you,' she confessed. 'I wouldn't have dared if your father hadn't prodded me into it.'

'Ah, yes, my father,' Ben said drily. 'Wait till I see him again! Of course, I realised he was conspiring with you. I'd never told him what happened between us, but he's a shrewd old man—he's very good at guesswork and he's never been afraid to take a gamble even when he is only guessing. He's not worried about interfering in other people's lives, either.'

'He's a darling,' Chloe protested. 'And he's very involved with you, Ben; it matters to him what happens to you. He really cares.'

'I know that or I'd have given him a flea in his ear long ago,' Ben said with resigned amusement.

'You didn't really ever suspect that he was interested in me himself, did you?' she asked and Ben shook his head, his eyes grim.

'Not really, although I did wonder for a second or two which of us you had in your sights.'

She blushed. 'There's no need to put it like that!'

His eyes cleared, turned mocking. 'It was a man hunt, admit it! You'd let me get away once but you weren't going to let me go again.'

She looked at him through her lashes uncertainly then smiled. 'One of us had to face facts. I knew I still loved you and I suspected you might feel the same, but you're so obstinate, you would have cut your nose off to spite your face, if I'd let you. I thought if I came to Venice I would give us both time to get to know each other again, and find out if . . .' Her voice trailed off and Ben's blue eyes surveyed her teasingly.

'If?' he prompted.

'If there was any chance,' she finished breathlessly.

'If there was any fire behind all the smoke,' Ben interpreted and her pulses beat fiercely at the look in his eyes.

'Chloe,' he whispered huskily and at that second someone tapped at the door. Ben scowled. 'I told them I wasn't to be disturbed!'

'It might be urgent,' Chloe said, hurriedly getting off his lap and tidying her hair with a hand that trembled slightly. Ben lay back in the chair, his face ironic as he watched her. She turned away and looked out of the window as he impatiently called: 'Yes, come in!'

The hotel secretary opened the door, looking apologetic. Ben regarded her with disfavour. 'I thought I told you I wasn't to be disturbed until I rang through?'

'I'm sorry, sir,' the girl stammered, holding out a flimsy envelope. 'But I thought this might be important.'

Ben held out his hand, still frowning. The girl scurried over to hand him the envelope, then vanished rapidly. Ben looked down, his long fingers automatically tearing the thin paper, extracting a telegraph form.

Chloe turned to face him, her face slightly apprehensive. 'I hate telegrams; they seem so ominous.'

He smiled at her. 'This is probably business; don't look so agitated.' He held out a hand. 'Come back here; I want you on my lap.' She obeyed, smiling, and he put an arm around her, kissing her hair. 'We'll have to send some telegrams ourselves soon. My father will want to know how well his conspiracy worked—or have you kept him fully informed all along?'

'Of course not! I haven't heard from him since I left London.'

'Was your mother in it? Yes, I suppose she was—well, at least some members of our families are on friendly terms. I can't promise to be very fond of that niece of yours. The best I can do is try not to tell her what I think of her. I don't imagine we'll see much of her now she's married, though.' A spark of wicked amusement lit his eyes. 'I suppose her husband wouldn't like a job in one of my more remote hotels—Hong Kong or Australia, maybe?'

Chloe sighed. 'I realise you'll never like Jilly.'

'Now there's an understatement for you!'

'She isn't as bad as you seem to think, Ben. When you get to know her . . .'

'I'm not planning to! Oh, don't worry, I'll be polite if I have to meet her, but try to keep her away from me as much as you can—there's a limit to how much pressure my temper can stand.'

Chloe couldn't deny that Jilly was a problem, she shrugged and nodded, then looked at the thin slip of paper he still held, unread.

'Hadn't you better read that? It might be urgent, you know.'

Ben unfolded it, saying: 'I suppose I might as well . . .' his voice cut off as if someone had corked his mouth.

'What's wrong?' Chloe asked anxiously, watching his face pass through a bewildering range of expressions.

'My God,' Ben breathed, reading the wire again.

'Ben, what is it? Bad news?' Chloe insisted, trying to read it too, her head twisted to see the short sentence which made up the message.

'My father,' Ben muttered, lifting his eyes to stare at her as if he didn't remember her. He was a funny colour; first he had turned pale, now he was dark red. Chloe's anxiety deepened.

'He isn't ill?' She had become so fond of Mr Haskell in the short time since she met him; she was stricken at the thought of anything happening to him.

'Ill?' Ben repeated on a rising note. 'Ill? No, he isn't ill but he does seem to have taken leave of his senses.' He sounded so angry that Chloe became even more disturbed. Surely Mr Haskell couldn't have sacked Ben? Or sold the company? What could he have done to make Ben look as though someone had just hit him on the head with a heavy object?

'What has he done?' she asked. Ben was breathing in a strange way now; Chloe stared at him in bewilderment.

'He's married your mother!' Ben choked and then she saw that he was not crying or in a furious temper, he was laughing helplessly. 'They've eloped—they're in Bermuda.'

Chloe snatched the telegraph, her jaw dropping. Her eyes skated hurriedly over what it said:

Married today. Honeymooning Bermuda. Love, Hetty and Joe.

She felt as though she had been kicked by a mule. Looking up, she stared at Ben, who was still grinning broadly.

'I can't believe it,' she whispered incredulously. 'Do you think it could be a joke?'

'An expensive one—it was sent from Bermuda. Look at the post office stamp at the top.'

Chloe stared blankly at it. 'Yes, you're right. But why didn't they tell anyone? Dorry can't know or she would have been on the phone to me and I haven't heard a peep out of her for days.' She looked up again, searching his face. 'You said they'd eloped—why do you say that?'

'I'm guessing—as you say, we haven't heard a whisper about this and if they had got married with the family all present there's no way they could have kept it a secret from us, is there? So they must have flown to Bermuda and got married there without telling a soul. They've eloped.' Ben started to laugh again, his wide shoulders shaking with helpless amusement.

'But why? Why do it secretly? Why not tell anyone?'

'Who knows? Because your mother thought it would be more romantic? Or because they didn't want any fuss? Or because at their age they thought people would laugh? It could be any one of a dozen reasons.'

'Dorry will be furious,' Chloe thought aloud, imagining her sister's reaction.

'Tough luck for Dorry, I don't see that it's any

of her business,' Ben said ruthlessly. 'Any more than it is anyone's affair if we decide to get married in the same way.' He looked thoughtfully at her. 'It certainly saves a lot of wear and tear on the nerves; no arrangements to make, no family hassle.'

'No white wedding dress, no veil, no bridesmaids,' Chloe said mournfully. 'No organ playing, no wedding cars with white ribbons, no reception.'

Ben eyed her with rueful amusement. 'Do I gather you want a big wedding?'

Chloe smiled airily. 'Oh, no! I'd simply hate to walk down the aisle wearing a ravishing dress made of silk and lace, and carrying a bouquet of roses and carnations, with white satin ribbons trailing from it. I've only been planning it ever since I was four years old and my cousin Julia wouldn't let me be her bridesmaid.'

Ben kissed her nose. 'Poor little mite! I see I'm doomed—condemned to a top hat and morning dress, I suppose?'

'I'm very conventional, that's how I've always seen it,' Chloe admitted with a demure look. 'A tall, handsome stranger waiting at the altar . . .'

'Stranger is right,' Ben said with a crooked smile. 'We really must try to get to know one another after we're married.'

Chloe looked down at the telegraph, her brow wrinkling. 'Do you think they do? They've rather rushed into it, haven't they?'

'Maybe they don't feel they have much time left,' Ben said.

'Gather ye roses while ye may,' Chloe murmured, nodding. 'Yes, I suppose it is a point of view.'

'My God,' Ben said, his eyes widening. 'Do you realise—I'm your stepbrother now.'

Chloe sat up, gasping. 'That hadn't occurred to me. So you are. Do you think it will make any difference, legally?'

'It won't be incest,' Ben said, grinning. 'No, of course it won't—but it is going to sound very funny on the wedding invitations. How on earth will we phrase it? Darling, are you certain you won't change your mind and consider eloping? It would save a lot of trouble.'

The 'phone rang and he glowered at it. 'Now what? Why have they put a call through? Don't tell me your mother has changed her mind?' He leaned over, still holding Chloe by the waist, and lifted the receiver. 'Yes?' he asked tersely.

Chloe softly nibbled the lobe of his ear and heard him give a husky little murmur of laughter, then he listened to whoever was on the other end of the 'phone and said calmly: 'Tell her that Miss Tyrrell will ring her back in half an hour, she's otherwise occupied at the moment.' He replaced the receiver as Chloe lifted her head in surprise at hearing her own name.

'Who was that? Not my mother?'

'No, your sister,' Ben said, amused. 'No doubt in a state of hysteria after getting a telegram from Bermuda.'

Chloe couldn't help laughing. 'Poor Dorry, I ought to talk to her before she goes beserk.'

'Later,' Ben said with husky impatience, pulling her towards him. 'We have more important things to discuss,' he whispered as his mouth came down to meet her lips, but they did not need words to say what their bodies were expressing with such urgency and fire, and the room was silent for a very long time.

Here's how to get this special offer from Harlequin!

OCTOBER
TREASURY EDITION
COUPON

As simple as 1...2...3!

1. Each month, save one Treasury Edition coupon from your favorite Romance or Presents novel.
2. In four months you'll have saved four Treasury Edition coupons (only one coupon per month allowed).
3. Then all you have to do is fill out and return the order form provided, along with the four Treasury Edition coupons required and $1.00 for postage and handling.

Mail to: Harlequin Reader Service

In the U.S.A.
2504 West Southern Ave.
Tempe, AZ 85282

In Canada
P.O. Box 2800, Postal Station A
5170 Yonge Street
Willowdale, Ont. M2N 6J3

RT1-C-2

Please send me my FREE copy of the Janet Dailey Treasury Edition. I have enclosed the four Treasury Edition coupons required and $1.00 for postage and handling along with this order form.

(Please Print)

NAME_____

ADDRESS_____

CITY_____

STATE/PROV._____ ZIP/POSTAL CODE_____

SIGNATURE_____

This offer is limited to one order per household.

This special Janet Dailey offer expires January 1986.

SUPPLIES LIMITED

H·A·R·L·E·Q·U·I·N

FIRST·CLASS
Sweepstakes

OFFICIAL RULES

1. NO PURCHASE NECESSARY. To enter, complete the official entry/order form. Be sure to indicate whether or not you wish to take advantage of our subscription offer.

2. Entry blanks have been preselected for the prizes offered. Your response will be checked to see if you are a winner. In the event that these preselected responses are not claimed, a random drawing will be held from all entries received to award not less than $150,000 in prizes. This is in addition to any free, surprise or mystery gifts which might be offered. Versions of this sweepstakes with different prizes will appear in Preview Service Mailings by Harlequin Books and their affiliates. Winners selected will receive the prize offered in their sweepstakes brochure.

3. This promotion is being conducted under the supervision of Marden-Kane, an independent judging organization. By entering the sweepstakes, each entrant accepts and agrees to be bound by these rules and the decisions of the judges, which shall be final and binding. Odds of winning in the random drawing are dependent upon the total number of entries received. Taxes, if any, are the sole responsibility of the prize winners. Prizes are nontransferable. All entries must be received by August 31, 1986.

4. The following prizes will be awarded:

    (1) Grand Prize: Rolls-Royce™ *or* $100,000 Cash!
    (Rolls-Royce being offered by permission of Rolls-Royce Motors Inc.)

    (1) Second Prize: A trip for two to Paris for 7 days/6 nights. Trip includes air transportation on the Concorde, hotel accommodations...PLUS...$5,000 spending money!

    (1) Third Prize: A luxurious Mink Coat!

5. This offer is open to residents of the U.S. and Canada, 18 years or older, except employees of Harlequin Books, its affiliates, subsidiaries, Marden-Kane and all other agencies and persons connected with conducting this sweepstakes. All Federal, State and local laws apply. Void in the province of Quebec and wherever prohibited or restricted by law. Winners will be notified by mail and may be required to execute an affidavit of eligibility and release, which must be returned within 14 days after notification. Canadian winners will be required to answer a skill-testing question. Winners consent to the use of their name, photograph and/or likeness for advertising and publicity purposes in conjunction with this and similar promotions without additional compensation. One prize per family or household.

6. For a list of our most current prize winners, send a stamped, self-addressed envelope to: WINNERS LIST, c/o Marden-Kane, P.O. Box 10404, Long Island City, New York 11101